DEADLY IN PINK

A CYBERPUNK NOVELLA

MATTHEW A. GOODWIN

Independently published via KDP

ISBN Number 978-1-7340692-1-1

Editor: Bookhelpline.com

Original cosplay design and model: Jenifer Ann

Photographer: David Love

Cover design: Christian Bentulan

CHAPTER 1

Ynna lay on the ground, tasting blood and seeing red. She would die the way she had lived, as garbage on the street. Her palms flat on the cement, she tried to raise her body and pick herself up. She sputtered, crimson exploding from her mouth and nose. Her knee scraped against the ground as she tried to move.

"You want more?" one of the five thugs asked her and laughed maniacally. "Killian was right about her."

She heard a laugh from one of the others. Her suspicions were confirmed. She had assumed he had sent them, but now she *knew* this wasn't just some random act. She bent, trying to force her body from the earth. One of her hands was broken, she knew, and pain shot through her as she tried to use it.

She thought about everything that had brought her to this place. She knew where it had all started, the true root of this beating.

"ONE THING BEFORE LUNCH," Ynna's mother, Karen, had said,

glancing over absently before returning to her palmscreen to check her feed.

"Ugh, mom, I want the eyeliner *and* foundation," Ynna groused. Her friends, such as they were, had spent the previous day mocking her makeup, and she knew she couldn't return to school without an upgrade. The words had stung, and now she could look great for tomorrow if her mom just let her buy both.

"Just one!" Karen barked, not even sparing a glance in her daughters' direction. Even at fifteen, Ynna saw the absurdity of it: they were rich. Her mom had the cart hovering at her side, filled to the brim with things she would use once and never think about again—or never even use once.

Shopping was one of the few activities Ynna and her mother enjoyed together. Brick and mortar stores had gone extinct for a time, with most retailers switching over exclusively to online ordering and drone delivery. But Friendlander's Department Store had stemmed the tide, banking on those like Ynna's mother who wished to make shopping an event rather than a necessity. They offered finger foods and drinks as shoppers moved throughout the floor. Local bands played soft music for ambiance, and workers littered the floor with samples or to answer questions.

Ynna looked at the two items, trying to choose. She glanced up, seeing the black domes she knew to contain cameras. None were close, and the counter shielded her waist. Though it was the weekend, she was dressed in her school uniform. Her father insisted that she always be adorned in the pleated skirt and white shirt with school crest whenever she left the house.

When she argued that she didn't want to wear it outside of school, he always repeated, "You attend a prestigious academy, and you should represent it with pride."

She hated it. The school. The uniform. Her friends. All of it.

His insistence made it feel like she was little more than a

trophy—something he could show off and parade around rather than a daughter he valued.

She smirked, pressing her body against the counter and sliding the eyeliner into her waist.

Her heart raced as she did it.

It was exhilarating.

She pulled the hem of her shirt out slightly so it would cover the small tube entirely. She glanced around. There were no alarms, no guards rushing over, just the normal bustle of the store.

Ynna sighed, smiled, and turned to her mother. "I'll take this," she said, presenting the foundation with pride.

"Good for you," her mother said, uninterested, waving a hand to the basket.

Ynna milled about the store excitedly as she waited for her mother. She watched the holoprojected models stride about the brightly lit shop, looking fabulous and beautiful. The clothes the models wore looked garish and almost absurd to Ynna, but she longed for a style all her own. Her eyes followed as they strutted down the aisles, passing through customers until her mother tapped her on the shoulder.

"Can we go?" Karen asked impatiently as though it was Ynna who had been holding them up.

The cart that followed Ynna's mother was synched to her palmscreen. It charged to her as they placed items in it, eliminating any need to stop at a register. As they moved to exit the store, Ynna heard the sound she had dreaded.

Her heart pounded, and her hands began to shake as the alarm blared.

Karen turned a withering glare on her daughter. "Marina, what did you do?"

Ynna threw her hands up in false innocence, but her mother saw right through it. She always hated it that her mother persisted in calling her by her given name even after Ynna begged her to stop.

A fat, weary-looking Carcer Corporation security guard hustled over, hands on his belt to keep it from sliding down his body. He huffed as he approached them. It was clear to both women that he did not have to get up from his desk very often.

He puffed, "What's going on here?"

"What's going on here," Karen said, reading the badge clipped to his belt, "Gerald, is that your machine appears to be broken."

She said it with such self-righteous indignation that Ynna herself nearly believed it.

"Oh, no, ma'am," he stuttered. "If you set the alarm off, I need to check your bag."

Karen's eyes narrowed, and her lips curled into little more than an angry line bisecting her face. "You will do no such thing. I pay for the privilege to shop here, and I will not be harassed because your machinery is faulty."

She pressed her hand on Ynna's shoulder to keep her from shifting back through the door and setting off the alarm again.

"Ma'am," Gerald forced, stepping toward them. "Please, I just need to check your bag."

"Lay a hand on me or my child, and you will be lucky to get a job scrubbing toilets. We are premier, Saffron Tier customers, and I promise you the owners of this establishment value me much more than you," she threatened. The young guard looked terrified and confused.

"Ma'am, please. If I don't do the check, I could lose my job," he implored her.

She took a step closer and nearly whispered. "The operative word being "could." You *could* lose your job if you let me walk out of here unmolested, but you certainly *will* lose your job if you detain us any longer."

Gerald looked to Ynna pleadingly, but she was not going to help him. With a sigh, he said, "fine," and turned with his head hung.

"Holy shit, mom," Ynna squealed delightedly.

"And you," Karen hissed venomously, reaching down and snatching the eyeliner from her daughter's skirt before jamming it in her purse. "Did you think nothing about getting caught? About what it could do to our reputation? Do you even care about that?

"We have to represent this family with pride, and here you are thieving like some back-alley ruffian. I've never been so disappointed in you in all my life.

"And what's worse is that now I need to cancel our lunch so we can go home and tell your father what you've done!"

"No, mom," Ynna pleaded. She hated it when her mother got this way, but she feared her father worse. He was not shy with discipline, and she was terrified at what he would do to her when he heard this.

"Please, what, Marina?" Karen asked as she dragged her daughter like a child toward the bank of waiting cars.

"Please don't tell him," she begged, feeling her eyes begin to burn.

Karen thrust Ynna toward a cab and hired it quickly with her palm. The doors to the luxurious black vehicle opened, and Karen pushed her daughter inside. The car door quickly closed and took off to their home.

Karen produced the eyeliner and threw it at Ynna, "For this?"

Silence followed, neither speaking a word for the duration of the ride back to their palatial estate. The cab descended right onto the front lawn. Ynna was shocked. Her mother always insisted that they land on the pad at the rear of the house so the thrusters wouldn't damage the grass. This action, more than the words, made Ynna realize how truly angry her mother was.

As the door opened, Ynna could smell the torched grass and scorched earth. Karen all but yanked her daughter from the cab and toward the front door surrounded by ornate colonnades. She stomped them into the atrium as they heard sounds coming from the kitchen. Karen stalked through the hallway, designed to look like an art gallery with expensive paintings and statues lining the walls. As they entered the kitchen, Ynna nearly vomited as she saw her father, pants around his ankles, penetrating their robotic maid.

The day the extravagantly expensive maid had arrived to replace the mechanical looking drudge that had served as their housekeeper, her father had argued that he simply wanted a more human touch around the house. Ynna had shared her mother's suspicions as to his true motivations, and they were now realized.

"Melvin!" Karen shrieked and turned to Ynna. "Go to your room!"

Her father turned wild eyes on them and tapped his palm, freezing the naked maid in time.

Ynna didn't have to be asked twice and rushed upstairs, slamming her door. As disgusted as she was, she was also relieved that this new distraction might save her from the punishment she had so feared in the ride over.

She brought up the security feed on the screen in her room, flopping onto her bed to watch. In order to sneak out of the house to meet her friends, Ynna had hacked the security network—a trick all the girls used to avoid their overbearing parents. The girls in their little clique had sidled up to Rose, an unpopular girl who they knew had the computer chops to help them. They befriended her and, naturally, dropped her like a hot potato once she had given them what they needed.

She watched as her father buckled his belt and screamed, "What are you doing home?"

Karen cast an icy glare at him. "It shouldn't matter when I come home. I shouldn't find you fucking a robot!"

"You would rather I do like the other men I work with and take up with my secretary?" he said, throwing his hands up.

Karen hung her head with disgust. "Perhaps you could just keep it in your pants?" she offered patronizingly.

Melvin let out a snide laugh, placing his hand on the exposed buttock of the frozen, perfect, human-like robot. "This is a machine, Karen. Having sex with her is no different than masturbating."

Now it was Karen's turn to laugh. "You just called it, 'her,' you idiot."

"This is your fault anyway." Melvin hissed the accusation.

"Oh, of course, it is," Karen said with affected astonishment.

"If you could maybe just part your legs now and again, I wouldn't have to do this," he shouted by way of explanation.

"That's rich," Karen snarled. "I do everything for you, and you dare to tell me that this," she pointed a perfectly manicured finger at the robot, "is my fault!"

He snorted. "You call ordering the food we eat and spending all my money, 'doing everything?'"

"You have got some nerve," Karen said, loathing in every word.

Ynna watched the situation unfold in horror. She knew her parents were unhappy, knew that whatever love they had shared was long behind them, but she hadn't realized they hated each other.

She felt as though it was her fault. She fidgeted with the stolen eyeliner, guilt coursing through her. If she hadn't taken it, hadn't felt the need to have one more accessory, they would never have rushed home and caught him.

She wanted to hurry downstairs and try to take the blame, but when her father spoke next, she knew it was too late.

"Maybe it's time you left," Melvin said, gesturing to the door.

"Gladly," Karen agreed. "I'll send someone for my things."

"*Your* things?" he mocked. "The only thing of yours you will be taking is that financial burden playing video games upstairs."

"What?" Ynna heard herself ask aloud. She couldn't believe how her father thought of her. She had never considered herself close to him, but she never thought he believed her a burden. She felt as though she had been shot in the chest.

She felt herself stand and watched as though it was someone else jamming clothes and mementos into a backpack. Her feet padded along the lush white carpet as she entered her parents' room. She pressed the code into the lock on her mother's closet —a code she was not supposed to know. She threw as much as would fit into her bag, stuffing a jewelry box on top of fine dresses she yanked from the shelves.

She prayed her father wouldn't notice as she kicked off her shoes and replaced them with the heels her mother saved for only the finest galas.

Ynna would never know what possessed her to do this, never quite understand what instinct kicked in at that moment, but she would always look back on it with pride.

"Marina!" her mother called up from the base of the stairs. She zipped her backpack shut with difficulty, the tines straining against the fullness.

"Coming, mom," Ynna called back, sliding the closet door closed behind her. She ran on wobbly legs, shaken both by the moment and her unfamiliarity walking in heels.

Her parents both looked at her with red faces as she made her way to them. Her mother caught sight of the shoes instantly and had to restrain a smile. Her father took no note.

"We're leaving," Karen announced.

"Yes, mother," Ynna said.

"Do you have anything to say to your father?" Karen offered.

"Yes," Ynna said, turning a withering gaze on the man. "Fuck you, asshole."

To her surprise, he didn't seem angry. He simply gave her a wicked smile. "Exactly," he said, his face contorting with bile. "Get out of my house."

CHAPTER 2

The cab was still waiting for them on the front lawn.

Ynna wondered if her mother had known all along how this would play out.

They stepped in silently, Karen's eyes vacant and distant. The cab lifted, hovering in place, and Karen let her hand dangle over her palmscreen. It became clear to Ynna in a moment how desperate they had become. Destitute in the space of a moment.

Her mother input something, and the car began to move. The oppressive quiet hung heavy on them until Ynna could not stand it anymore.

"I'm so sorry!" she burst out and launched herself into her mother's arms. Karen seemed shocked at first, but pulled her daughter in and held her tight, stroking her hair.

"It's not your fault," she soothed.

"It is! It's all my fault," Ynna wailed.

Her mother kissed her head. "No, honey, it isn't. Your father and I have been careening toward this for a long time. If it hadn't happened today, it might have tomorrow. Or next week. Or, if I were unlucky, a year later."

"But mom, what will you do?" Ynna sobbed.

"We will be fine. I've been at the bottom before, and I can scrape my way out again. It's you I'm worried about," she whispered.

"I'll help! I'll do whatever I need to make this okay," Ynna promised.

"Oh, I know. I know you will try," Karen said with a little smile and kicked Ynna's foot. "You've already proven to be a smart young woman."

Ynna pulled back, the tears streaming down her face. "I did this, too," she said, pulling the backpack around and unzipping it to reveal the things she had rescued.

A smile of motherly pride crossed Karen's lips. "I never gave you credit for how clever you are."

Karen's eyes were wet now, too.

"So… what are we going to do?" Ynna asked, terrified as to what the answer could be.

"Start a new life, and with this," Karen pointed to the jewelry box, "you gave us a lifeline."

"I'm happy I did *something* right," Ynna said, still blaming herself for all of it.

"We will be okay," Karen assured her.

"So, what now?" Ynna asked.

"Now I have to find a place for us, and I need to find some work," Karen explained. Her matter of fact tone surprised Ynna. Her mother seemed so calm while she felt scared and confused. Her whole world had turned upside down in an instant, and she knew it would never be the same.

"Maybe uncle Stu can help us?" Ynna offered. He had always been kind to them, and he was one of the few family members who Ynna trusted.

Karen smiled weakly. "No. Your uncle is a sweet man, but he depends on your father for all he has. Stu only works at the firm because of him and will no doubt be helping your father strip us of everything before too long."

"Oh," Ynna said. The wheels of her mind were turning, grasping for any idea she could offer. "What about cousin Liz? She works at some biotech company. Maybe we could work with her?"

Her mother let out a shrill laugh. "Oh, honey, let me tell you about Elizabeth. She works as some kind of naked courier, working for chauvinists who have enough money to get away with anything. They use the guise of proprietary information to strip young women of their clothes and their dignity and parade around offices nude. It's a hard world and an especially hard world for women."

Ynna didn't understand what she was hearing. The people she thought she knew were nothing like what they had seemed, and she felt foolish and naïve. The world was also much grimmer than she had perceived from her estate. She wanted to press her mother for more information but couldn't find the words.

"Let me tell you something," Karen said, looking into Ynna's eyes with a seriousness she had never before seen. "This world is governed by money. We have lived the way we have because we had it. We won't now, and you will see what the world is like for the other ninety-nine percent. They are no better off than drudges. They work as cogs in a corporate machine that has put everything in your lap until now. I will do everything I can to keep you from becoming like your cousin, but you will have to learn very quickly that the world is a harsh and unfair place."

Ynna had never heard her mother speak like this. She seemed like a different person from the one she had known her whole life. Ynna had known her mother had not always been the wealthy debutante who had raised her. Now, she felt like she was seeing the woman who had existed before.

"So, where are we going?" Ynna asked, looking out the window of the cab to see a part of the city she didn't recognize. Gone were the luxurious homes and familiar skyscrapers. They were replaced by ramshackle structures that looked more like rubble than buildings.

"That's the thing, my love. I've thought about leaving your father for so long, but it wasn't until he said I should leave that I realized how alone I am," she said, deep sadness coating every word. "All of my friends are the acquaintances of wealth. Friends of lifestyle rather than substance. When we got in this cab, I understood for the first time that I am alone. I should have thought about where I would go after leaving him, rather than just the act of doing so."

Ynna's mouth hung open as she listened.

"What... what about Bette? You guys seem so close," Ynna offered. Even after hearing what her mom said about feeling alone, Ynna figured her closest friend might offer them help.

Karen dropped her head, long raven hair falling in front of her face. "She would take us in, and she would love it, but not for altruistic reasons. She would love the superiority. She would tell all the ladies at the club how we came to her in our time of need, rub it in their faces and mine. Smile as she pitied me. I would rather die in a gutter than live through the condescension." Karen's voice cracked as she said the last words.

Karen unfurled her palm and made a call. After two rings, an olive-skinned man with graying black hair appeared on the screen.

"Karen," he said, and it sounded more like a question than a greeting.

"Hello, Hector," Karen said.

"This is a blast from the past," he said with a confused smile, his English heavily accented.

"I'm by your place and need your help," Karen told him.

"You can have it, always," Hector said, his round face friendly and open.

THE CAB SET down on a crumbling landing pad, and Ynna had a difficult time stepping down. Loud music of accordions and trumpets blared from down the street, and the combined smell of petrol and open cooktops filled the air.

This part of the city was like a different world to Ynna. The streets were mobbed with citizens in threadbare outfits, sweaty and tired from hard labor. Ynna was nervous. She had never seen poverty before. She didn't understand that people lived this way.

People's eyes scanned the two women in their finery, and Ynna's hands began to shake. Before too long, the man from the screen appeared through the crowd and waved. Karen gave a wave back, acting completely at ease with their surroundings.

She hurried over and embraced the short, plump, middle-aged man who Ynna recognized as Hector.

"This is my daughter, Marina," Karen said.

"Ynna," her daughter corrected.

"Good to meet you," he said, extending a sweaty hand that Ynna reluctantly shook. She hoped he didn't notice as she wiped her hand against the side of her skirt.

"Come, come," he said, gesticulating wildly with his hands.

He turned and plodded down the bustling street. They moved through some people dancing as three older men played music and sang. They wore clothes that looked as though they had not been washed for some time, if ever, but also joyous smiles.

A young woman rushed over to them holding a robotic leg.

"Cheap, cheap," she told them before Hector waved her away. Ynna couldn't imagine a person wanting to get upgraded so desperately that they would purchase cybernetics from a street vendor.

She stayed close to her mother, who seemed to be reveling in the moment. Karen turned a kind eye on her daughter.

"You doing alright?" She whispered, seeing the nervousness.

"Sure," Ynna mustered, not knowing how she felt. Her life had changed so much in such a short time, and she had no idea how it would be progressing from here.

A man yelled to them from behind a cart with what Ynna could only imagine was meat cooking on the surface. His words were in a language Ynna did not recognize, and as he finished, a metal plate fused to his neck barked, "bacon-wrapped hot dogs," in a synthetic voice.

Karen looked from the man to Hector. "I see you are still too proud to get a translation mod."

Hector shot them a smirk. "Is not pride. I prefer to speak my own words in a broken language than let a computer speak for me."

Karen nodded slightly as Ynna considered his words. Having just witnessed the effects of modern technology on her father, she was heartened to hear that the man did not want to rely on it.

Hector guided them to a three-story building covered in spray-painted artistic renderings of citizens throwing rocks at Carcer officers.

"You can have the room of my sister," Hector offered them.

"That's very kind," Karen told him. "I will also need a job."

Hector scoffed as he put a key into a steel gate door. "My dear, everyone needs a job these days, but I may be able to help you."

"My friend, I will never be able to repay you for this," Karen said, placing a hand on his sweaty shoulder while he guided them up a flight of stairs.

Ynna nearly tripped on a loose thread from the worn carpet that lined the steps. She considered taking off the shoes but thought better of it as she noticed the jutting nails and staples that worked hard to keep the fabric in place.

They had to step over a man, eyes black, a cord extending from his head to a socket in the wall.

"Many prefer false reality to the world around them," Hector informed them. Karen did not seem surprised, but Ynna was aghast as she watched the man twitch and smelled the dry urine. She had known that people struggled outside of her sheltered existence, but she had never truly understood until now.

As Hector pushed his front door open, Ynna's mouth fell open as she realized he hadn't left it locked. Her house was a fortress, not only from without but from within as well. Even she couldn't access portions of her own home without codes.

They stepped onto the linoleum coated floor, yellowed and faded from where the light seeped in through torn curtains.

A small boy of about five stood on a step stool with a grill pan sitting atop a range in one hand and a spatula in the other. He grinned at them with pride as they entered.

"Making lunch, papa," he announced, turning to face them in an apron that was far too large for him and bore some corporate logo that Ynna did not recognize.

"Bueno. Good boy, Marco," Hector said.

"Jamón," he said as he flipped one of the sandwiches in the pan, sending cheesy grease spraying.

"Follow me," Hector said to the women and guided them to a room smaller than Ynna's closet at home. It was hot and cramped. A mattress lay on the floor with reasonably nice-looking bedding folded neatly on top. A fan wobbled overhead, looking poised to drop to the ground at any moment. Posters of soccer players without their shirts on were nailed into the cracked drywall, and a large television sat on the floor.

"Take some time to get settled and find me," Hector said, hooking a thumb over his shoulder.

Karen smiled graciously and closed the door. Ynna set down the backpack and sat on the floor, her mother sitting beside her and wrapping an arm over her shoulder.

"We are going to be okay," she said.

"You don't seem as thrown off by this as I would have expected," Ynna told her.

Karen let out a little chuckle. "I've known this day was coming, and this was how I grew up. This is how *most* people grow up. The world we were able to give you is just a fantasy for almost everyone. But, as I said, I've scraped my way up from the bottom before and can do it again."

"How will I get to school?" Ynna asked, flattening her skirt against her leg.

Karen grimaced, looking forlorn. "Oh, honey," she said, her eyes welling again.

"Oh," Ynna said. Her heart broke at the idea that she would likely never see her classmates again. She knew her friends to be vain and cruel, but they were also the only people she had. The boys in her class were mean and pigheaded, but she still liked to compete for their affections.

Everything she knew had changed in an instant, and she hated herself for stealing the eyeliner. Despite her mother's words, she couldn't shake the knowledge that if she had just put it down, just bought the one thing, they would be sitting in a fine restaurant right now rather than squatting on a floor.

She watched as specks of dust fluttered in a beam of light cast through a hole in a curtain. "So, what will I do now?"

"I won't be able to afford to send you to school, and we won't get anything from your father, so you will probably have to do VR classes once we can afford a rig," Karen said. She looked to her daughter with a smile. "But you are already so smart. You will be able to do great things."

"Thanks, mom," Ynna said. She had never liked school, finding herself bored in class. She did well on tests and projects, but they never excited her. The most interested in learning she had ever been was watching the girl they had tricked into hacking their homes. Ynna had found herself fascinated watching as the security systems fell.

Even though she had not enjoyed school, she felt lost without the prospect of attending. It had been her life's trajectory, and now she needed to find a new one.

This time, she struggled to assure herself, it would be of her own design.

Ynna and her mother changed into some casual attire she had brought from the house and walked back into the living room. Hector sat on a couch with a beer in hand, eating one of the sandwiches his son had cooked up. The kid rushed over to them with a plate in hand.

"Eat!" he exclaimed, and the women grabbed the warm food gratefully. Globbed cheese, frozen in time from contact with the pan stuck to the sides. Ynna was accustomed to fine, small bites presented just so, and she looked at the sandwich dubiously. Not wanting to be rude, she took a bite. Flavor from the meat, cheese, and spread filled her mouth, and her eyes went wide with delight.

It was delicious.

She devoured the whole thing and scooped another off the plate, much to the delight of the kid who looked between them and his father for approval.

"It's wonderful," she told him, her mouth full, grease dripping down her arm.

He beamed. "Hear that, Papa?"

"Good job," he told his son and slapped the couch next to him. "Ladies, join me."

They walked over and sat on the couch, springs groaning under their slight weight. He produced two beers from a cooler next to him and held them out by the necks. Ynna looked to her mother for permission.

"Marina, I'm no fool," she said, and Ynna grinned, grabbing a beer and opening it quickly. She had drunk alcohol and taken drugs, but never with her parents' knowledge. It wasn't a surprise to her that her mother had known, but she realized then that little would surprise her anymore.

As she sipped at her drink, Hector shifted on the couch to face them. "Karen, mi amiga, I spoke to a man who may be able to get you a job. It is not much, but it will pay. You can stay here until you get back on your feet.

"In the morning, you will meet the man, and I will take Ynna to sell those shoes I saw her wearing. It will help, I think."

"We actually have quite a few things to sell," Karen said and looked back at her daughter with pride.

"You are smart," he told Karen, who shook her head.

"My daughter is smart," Karen said.

"Excelente," Hector said, smiling his big friendly grin. He turned his eyes on Ynna. "You will do well out here."

"She will," Karen agreed. "But we will need to get her into school."

"Tomorrow, we will ask Killian about an access rig," Hector assured her.

CHAPTER 3

The rest of the afternoon passed uneventfully. Hector regaled Ynna with stories of her mother before she was the woman she now knew. She learned more about Karen in a few hours than she had in her whole life. The exhaustion of the day caught up with both women, and they crawled into bed as soon as the sun set.

Ynna was awakened throughout the night by yelling and the sound of gunfire (as she would later learn). Nights had been so quiet at home, and here, in the real city, she came to understand how the night truly sounded. She was groggy when Hector knocked on the door, saying, "Is time."

She rubbed her face, feeling slimy and gross.

"Think I have time to shower?" Ynna asked, not sure if her mother would know the answer.

Karen shook her head slightly. "Maybe, but water isn't cheap."

Ynna was confused by that. "Isn't water free?"

"Nothing is free." Her mother chuckled.

"Ugh," she groaned, "so I can't even shower."

"Once we can pay our own way, of course," Karen explained,

leaving Ynna to realize she would have to feel sticky all day long. It was hot in the room despite the threatening fan.

Karen stood and stretched. "I'm going to change if you want to ask Hector about your day," she suggested, and Ynna nodded.

She stood. Her body felt sore and achy. She made her way out to the living room and found Hector sitting on the couch with a cup of coffee. Like her, he wore the same clothes as the day before, and she assumed he had slept in them as well.

"Young lady, ready for the day ahead?" he asked. She appreciated that, despite how little he seemed to have, he was eternally upbeat.

"Yep," Ynna told him, holding forth the backpack. "Packed up some things we can sell today."

"Good," he said, taking a sip of his steaming drink and turning back to look at the television as he spoke. "I will be your guide for the day. You learn much. Café on the pot. You want?"

"Sure," she said.

After so many late nights with her friends, she had taken to drinking coffee most mornings. Though her father always groused that with all the cream and sugar, what she drank was more like, "A liquified candy bar."

"Mug's on the counter," Hector said, pointing while not taking his eyes from the screen. The newscasters were prattling on about the unseasonable heat in the district.

Ynna poured herself a mug and, seeing nothing to add to the drink, joined Hector on the couch. She had been unable to get a straight answer from her mom, so she asked him, "What do you do for a living?"

He tried to cover a smirk with his mug, but Ynna saw it.

"This y that," he said, as obnoxiously cryptic as her mother had been.

Ynna fumed. "I'm not a child. You know?"

"No, no," Hector laughed lightly. "First day out here, you are a pinche newborn."

Ynna wanted to throw the coffee in his face. She hated being talked to like she was less-than, hated when teachers and adults felt the need to speak to her like a kid. But looking around the room and thinking about the previous day, she had to admit to herself that he had a point.

The only thing she did seem to know was that she knew nothing of the world.

She took a sip of the coffee and nearly gagged but forced the warm liquid down. "So, you'll teach me?"

He turned his large, chestnut eyes on her. She noted that one eye was colored slightly different and suspected that it might be cybernetically enhanced. If that was the case, with how close the color match was, it wasn't some cheap version. If her suspicions were correct, she found it amusing that he would take *some* technological enhancements.

He smiled. "Yes, I teach you."

Ynna smiled, too.

AFTER HE HAD GIVEN Karen instructions on where to go, he led Ynna out into the street. Even early in the day, it was warm. The people who weren't on their way to or from work sat at street-front cafes, enjoying the morning. Others clambered up scaffolding to repair the side of a building, and Ynna was struck by the fact that people were doing the work rather than the drudges she was accustomed to seeing.

As they walked, a heavyset blond man hurried over to Hector and whispered something in his ear as they shook hands. He hustled off as quickly as he had appeared. When Ynna shot Hector a quizzical look, he simply grinned like a Cheshire Cat.

"Pays to have friends," he told her, unintentionally emphasizing the word, "pays."

At that moment, Ynna came to understand that there was much more to this friendly man than she had assumed. This sense only grew as she watched the way people looked at him. It wasn't the fear her father's underlings showed, nor the reverence her friends showed when some celebrity mom showed up at school, but something else.

Respect.

She saw it in the eyes of those they passed, and the slight head nods. She had been too scared the day before to notice, but now it was clear as day.

Walking by his side, she liked the feeling it gave her, and she vowed to watch him and learn.

THEY APPROACHED a store with barred windows and display racks set in front with electronic equipment and various other used items chained down. A sign above the door read, "Knight Takes Pawn Shop," in flickering neon lights.

A bell rang as they stepped through the door. Displays flanked them on either side, and racks of cheap-looking guns lined the walls. At the rear of the shop, a gaunt, pale man watched a movie on his palmscreen. He had pulled his long brown hair into a greasy ponytail, and his hands were dirty— black crud caught under every fingernail. He wore what appeared to be a new leather jacket, studded with short metal spikes.

Hector cleared his throat, and the man's eyes rolled up to them before stopping on Ynna. He scanned her body in a way that made her skin crawl. Boys had often gazed at her, complimenting her body and big eyes, but no one had ever leered at her the way this man did. She shifted uncomfortably and crossed her arms in front of herself.

The man smiled with thin lips, exposing yellowed teeth. "If she's a relief aide, I'm not sure I can afford her, but I'll sure as shit try." He spoke with a slight brogue that Ynna would have found charming on someone else.

Hector's face grew grim, and his tone, threatening. "Not for you, Killian."

The man raised his hands defensively. "Just saying," he stated, not taking his eyes off her.

Ynna was disgusted but knew she needed to play nice.

Hector pointed to the backpack. "She's got some things to sell, and I want a good deal."

"Oh, she'll get a good deal," Killian said. Every word that left his lips had a sexual undertone.

Hector looked at Ynna. "I'm going to look around in the back," he told her and turned back to Killian. "Anything she no like, and I'll pull your arm off."

Killian shot him a crude smile, "my arm's not the thing I want pulled."

Hector stepped forward, his short frame menacing. "Killian, I swear."

"Just playing around," Killian said with an affected kind tone. He pressed a button, and a large metal door behind him opened.

Hector looked to Ynna as he stepped behind the counter. "He does anything, you just call out."

Ynna nodded. Though she wasn't thrilled about being left with the man, she appreciated that Hector trusted her to be left alone. As he disappeared into the back, Killian continued to stare. From the way Hector spoke to the man, she understood that this was how he treated the girls who came to his shop. She had seen enough creeps in her day to know that he got off on the uncomfortable feeling he elicited from women.

So, she smiled. With a broad, winning grin, she thrust her hand out and said, "I'm Ynna."

The gambit paid off. Killian looked confused for a moment and stepped back, wiping his hand on his pant leg before taking hers.

"Killian," he said, regaining his composure. "You're new here?"

"Yessir," she said with such a forced bubbly affect as to be laughable.

"And—and you have things to sell?" he asked, clearly unable to read her. Where her discomfort had given him strength, her affability clearly put him ill at ease. She was proud of herself for reading him so quickly and getting a leg up on the situation.

"Right again," she told him, opening her bag and laying the contents on the counter.

"This'll do," he said as he opened the jewelry box to examine the items.

Ynna smirked. "I see a hand drop below the counter, and I'll have Hector back here before you can blink," she told him with a wink.

He seemed impressed and smiled. "Clever girl."

"I'm a lot more than clever," she said, drawing on the same surprising confidence that had motivated her to grab the items she was now selling.

"You know," he said as if an idea was occurring to him for the first time.

"What's that?" Ynna asked, cocking her head to the side.

"Well," he said, leaning forward and speaking in a conspiratorial tone, "I may have a way for you to earn a little pocket money."

Ynna wished he would get to the point, but she played along. "I'm listening."

"I employ a few slip-gibbets—young people, such as yourself, who help me," here he paused implicitly, "redistribute wealth."

"That so?" she asked, interested for the first time in what the man was saying.

Killian wiggled his eyebrows. "It is."

"Redistribute from other pockets to yours?" she put bluntly.

"I think you have the wrong idea," he falsely protested, but tapped his finger to his nose and winked.

"I *could* use some extra money," she said with a devilish grin. She knew her mother would never approve, but she didn't care. She wanted to carve out her own place in the world. Her life had been on rails until yesterday, and now she wanted to know what her capabilities were.

"I thought you might," Killian said. "Lose the old man and come visit me someday."

"Right," she said dubiously. His use of "old man" seemed odd to her. If anything, Killian seemed much older than Hector, but that may have been simply a low life prematurely aging his features. She also worried what coming here without a protector would mean. She had taken a self-defense class for young women offered through her school but worried what Killian might try if he had her alone.

Even wearing a loose-fitting top as she was, he had hardly taken his eyes from her chest since she walked in, and she knew she needed to be smart if she planned to deal with him alone.

"So," she said, changing the subject, "how much for all this?"

He looked at the items and pursed his lips. "Ten thousand."

"Ten thousand?" She scoffed. "Those shoes alone are worth ten times that!"

He clicked his tongue. "A thing is only worth what someone is willing to pay, and out here, people don't have much."

"Still, I'm pretty sure Hector said to give me a good deal," Ynna protested.

"I'm not sure you know what a good deal is," Killian said, his voice rife with condescension.

"I know it's not ten," Ynna said, her tone unwavering.

"Fine, I'll do twenty, and you'll be happy to take it," Killian said as though he was giving her the deal of a lifetime. She knew he was probably right that people wouldn't pay much for what she was selling, but she also knew how much they had cost in the first place. She wasn't going to let him buy everything she had for next to nothing.

"How about fifty?" she asked, pained that she had to press for so little. Her prom dress alone had cost more than that.

Killian laughed. A gross, dismissive sound that reminded her of what he truly was.

"I'm sorry, did I fucking stutter? Pretty sure I said fifty." The words left her mouth with a surety that impressed her.

Killian groaned. "I'll hardly turn a profit."

Ynna pointed a proud finger. "But you will turn a profit."

She had him. "Fine," he conceded. "Fifty for the lot."

Ynna wanted to push him, wanted him to see that she was smart and capable. More than that, she wanted to show herself. "Right, fifty for the lot, except this." She unfurled a long pearl necklace from the jewelry box. She had seen him eyeing it and knew he wouldn't want to part with it. But she wanted something she could return to her mother. Something they could hold on to as a reminder of where they had come from.

Killian moaned. "That wasn't the deal."

"I'm altering the deal," Ynna grinned.

"Fine," Killian said. "But that's it, and I expect you to bring this level when you run jobs for me."

Ynna was so proud of herself, she wanted to do a dance. But she simply smiled and put the pearls in her pocket. "Oh, I will."

HECTOR TOOK ONLY a short while longer in the back and emerged with a handful of things that Ynna did not recognize. She did see a large black box tucked under his arm with the words, "VR Education II," scrawled on the side. During the pandemic which engulfed the world generations earlier, city dwellers were forced to stay in their homes to stem the spread of the illness. Schools became digital only classrooms to deter cross-contamination and even when the pandemic was resolved, the change stuck. Some brick and mortar schools like the one Ynna had attended reopened but most had not. She assumed that the headset would be somewhat inexpensive as the technology was outdated, long ago replaced with lenscreens or cybernetic eyes which would feed the classroom right into one's brain.

"Your little friend robbed me blind," Killian sneered.

Hector smiled. "That, I am happy to hear."

"I'll bet you are," Killian murmured.

Hector looked at Ynna. "He pay you?"

She held up the cash chip with the value digitally displayed on the side. Hector's smile broadened.

"Your school is my treat," he told her as he heaved the stuff onto the counter. "As thank you to your mama."

"You're already doing so much," Ynna pointed out, not that she wanted to pay for the rig.

"The kindness she showed me once can never be repaid," Hector told her. She desperately wanted to ask about their history but knew better. Her mom had been cagey and changed the subject, and she knew he would do the same.

. . .

BACK AT THE APARTMENT, Ynna found herself unbearably bored by the curriculum of the digital classroom. The academy she had attended had been so advanced that this low-level education was painfully uninteresting. When the school day ended, she found the apartment empty save for a skinny cat sleeping on the couch next to her. She hadn't seen it enter and hardly wanted to move when she prodded it to make sure it was alive. Hector had excused himself as soon as they had arrived, and it was another hour before her mom came striding in.

"I got a job," Karen announced.

Ynna beamed. "That's great, mom."

"It's not much, and it's obvious the owner of the diner is just doing it as a favor to Hector, but I'll take it," Karen said. "You sell our belongings?"

Ynna passed her mom the chip, which Karen flipped over in her hand, seeing the value. "More than I expected."

"I have a way with people," Ynna boasted.

Her mother put a hand on her knee. "I know you do."

Karen continued to show pride in Ynna that she wished she had experienced before leaving their old life. In a small way, Ynna was happy about what had happened. She felt a sense of purpose and skill she had never before known and saw a side of her mother she didn't know existed. She was scared for their future, but also hopeful and excited.

"How was school, did you try it today?" Karen asked, pointing to the headset by Ynna's side.

"I did. It was good," she lied, not wanting to disappoint her mother.

"That's wonderful!" Karen smiled. "It sounds like I'll be working long and odd hours, so I may not see you as much as I'd like."

Ynna gave her a soft smile and chuckled. "Mom, I've seen you more in the last two days than in the last two years."

A pained expression crossed her mother's face. "I know, honey. But our new life begins today, and I'll make sure to see you as much as I can."

She wrapped her daughter up in an embrace that lasted a long time.

The skinny cat looked up lazily, stood and stretched, its long body arching, and it's hair standing on edge. It began to purr, and it moved to the warm headset on the couch. As it nuzzled its muzzle against the electronic device, the red light on the side of the rig turned green, indicating that the headset was in contact with a person.

Ynna grinned.

CHAPTER 4

It wasn't long before Ynna understood the rhythm of life in the apartment. Hector and Marco would be up before the sun and, though both son and father would be out most of the day, they would return home for family dinner every night. Most nights, Hector would go back out after eating. When he didn't, he would spend his time showing the two kids how to fend for themselves and encouraging them to work out in the apartment. Most evenings, after practicing their moves, Marco would play video games with Ynna until they could barely keep their eyes open.

Karen worked long shifts and was able to do little more than sleep in the times between. Ynna had known her mother to do little more than shop and eat, and it came as a shock to see her transition so easily into a life of labor. Ynna would occasionally go down the street to the diner to visit and eat but spent most of her days alone in the apartment, struggling to stay awake during her virtual classes.

Midmornings, the cat, who Hector simply called "Gato," would appear through the window after a night of chasing the rats that clicked and chattered in the walls. Ynna began saving scraps of food and would feed the cat who, after being sated, would curl up next to her and sleep all day in a fluffy curl.

It was a while before she was brave enough to attempt what she had in mind. She signed into her class and removed the headset instantly. It vibrated slightly to alert the user that they were in non-compliance, and she quickly set it down on the rump of Gato, who looked up briefly at the shaking device before falling back to sleep. The vibration stopped when it came in contact with the body heat. Ynna smirked, thinking herself terribly clever—though she would later learn that this was one of the oldest tricks in the hooky playbook.

She wanted to test the system before trying it out for real, so she spent the day as a detective in Victorian London on Marco's console. Playing video games with the young man had reinvigorated her love of escapism, and she began to understand why so many chose the digital world rather than the one before them.

In her life as a spoiled rich daughter of an affluent father, she spent her time trying to one-up her friends with exotic selfies, more concerned with looking like she was having fun than actually having it. Here, she felt the need to share nothing, nor any desire to see what all her "friends" (who had since gone silent) were up to. Her father had cut off service to her and Karen's palmscreens anyway, and it was no longer a luxury she cared to pay for.

After discovering that the butler had been wrongfully accused of stealing the dowager's necklace, Ynna felt the headset beside her buzz, and she blinked back to reality. She hit the pause button, and the holoprojected world of the game vanished, leaving her sitting in the squalid room. She popped on the headset and saw the words CLASS COMPLETE next to a green checkmark displayed within.

She smirked.

She would have between eight and sixteen hundred the following day to explore. She was still nervous about seeing Killian without her protector, but her excitement for action made her feel at ease. She had outwitted him on their first meeting and knew she could do so again.

She also wanted money. Something bound Hector to her mother, but he owed Ynna nothing and was still kind and generous to her. She didn't want to have to ask for things from him or her mom anymore. She had to admit to herself that she missed shopping, missed having the means to scroll through images of items and pick something out for herself. Hector and her mother had both taken her to the all-in-one superstore to buy things, but it left her feeling meek and beholden.

The girl who desired luxury items died in the cab ride to this part of the city. Now, she wanted practical things she purchased for herself.

Determined, she left the apartment to walk the streets alone for the first time.

Her confidence wavered quickly when a large woman bumped into her intentionally and snarled something under her breath. Ynna decided to stop for liquid courage at a small refrigerated cart selling shots of spiced rum. The ancient man looked at her and smiled, picking up one of the small, dirty glasses in a metal hand with just two roboict fingers.

"On the house for a friend of Hector," he wheezed.

"Cheers," she answered with forced confidence, lifting the glass and gulping down the brown liquid. It burned down her throat, and she sputtered a cough. The old man laughed lightheartedly. She set the glass down with more force than she intended, rattling the glasses.

Head swimming, she regretted the decision to have a drink. She moved through the crowded streets toward the shop.

Standing before the racks of items, she took a deep breath, the taste of booze swimming in her mouth.

The bell rang, and Killian gave her a devious grin as she entered.

"I knew I could get you to come," he said with his usual disgusting undertone.

Ynna strode to the counter and smiled. "Here for work."

"Oh, I'll put you to work." He smirked and began tapping at his palm. "Let's make you some friends."

HE ASKED after Hector while they waited, Ynna providing evasive non-answers to all his questions. She came to understand that though they worked together, there was no love lost between the two. She tried to get more answers as to what exactly Hector did for money, but Killian was as forthright with Ynna as she was with him.

Before too long, a young woman entered, about Ynna's age and very pretty. She had a cool look, wearing sprayed-on leather pants, a denim vest over an exposed bra, and dark makeup on her face. Ynna felt the familiar pang of jealousy she experienced when she would hang out with the pretty girls at school. Ynna knew she was attractive, her parents genetically designing her flawless features in utero, but this girl had the confidence which Ynna lacked.

She strode in and posed, crossing her arms judgmentally as she appraised Ynna. "New meat?" she asked.

"Whitney," Killian said, "this is Ynna."

Whitney cocked her head. "Weird name," she observed as though it was the first time this point was made. "I'm Whitney."

Ynna extended a hand. "Nice to meet you."

Whitney did not move to take the hand. "I'm good." She turned to Killian. "Little rich girl thinks she can hang with us?"

"If I say she can, she can," Killian told her.

"We'll see," Whitney said in a voice that clearly expressed her doubt.

"Let me know how she does," Killian ordered, and Whitney nodded grudgingly.

Though she knew the girl disliked her and clearly wished she would go away, Ynna wanted to impress her. She needed friends outside the apartment, and she hoped that she could turn Whitney around.

As they exited the building, both girls ignored Killian as he called after them, "I love to see you go, but I love to watch you leave."

Whitney shook her head. "That's not even the fucking saying."

"He's a dimwit anyway," Ynna said.

"Dimwit who pays," Whitney corrected.

"He creep on you?" Ynna asked, trying to sound conversational, but the words sounded stilted as they left her mouth.

"Sure, but who wouldn't? I mean, look at me," she said with a sweeping hand gesture.

There it was—that confidence Ynna so desperately wanted. Whitney turned an eye on her. "You're no slouch, though. I'm sure the boys love to put you away wet."

Ynna stifled her shock. The brazen bluntness of the girl's words was not like anything she was used to. In the circles she was used to running in, saying what you meant was a social faux pas.

Ynna dropped her head and mumbled, "I mean, I do okay."

"I'm sure you do more than okay, and I'll tell you right now, I'm not in the market for any competition."

Ynna looked her over, watching her perfect ass shift as she walked. She tried to think of just the right thing to say, trying, "You have nothing to worry about with me. I mean, look at you."

Without thinking, she reached out and slapped the girl on her behind. Instantly, she regretted taking that drink again. Whitney wheeled around, but rather than the anger Ynna anticipated, she was smiling.

"You've got fire in you, girl," Whitney said, and for the first time, Ynna felt as though she was making headway.

"I try," Ynna smirked.

"You smell like fucking sauce," Whitney noted with a raised eyebrow.

"That a problem?" Ynna asked, feeling more at ease with her.

Whitney smiled. "Oh, hell no. Just an observation. I prefer the synth stuff myself, but to each her own."

Ynna had dabbled in the lab-created recreational drugs but had found them too powerful. The loss of control made her uncomfortable, and she had found it boring to lay on couches in palatial estates tripping.

"Alright, princess. Ready for a whole new world?" Whitney mocked as they approached an abandoned factory.

"Sure," Ynna grumbled, not surprised that the young woman had reverted to her patronizing tone.

The brick building was massive, the heavy doors frozen open with rust. Tents and tarps were propped against machinery unused for an age. The vaulted roof was lined with cracked and broken windows. People milled about lazily, exchanging trinkets and stories.

"What is this place?" Ynna heard herself asking.

Whitney chuckled. "People just call it The Press. Used to be someplace they printed stuff on paper. Home away from home for some, straight-up home for others."

"Oh," Ynna said as she passed an open tent with a man snoring loudly in nothing but ripped underpants. He gripped an injector with an affixed empty vial in one hand that had fallen open. Scars and open sores covered his body.

The two young women turned many heads, but no one approached them.

Whitney seemed to read Ynna's mind. "We are safe here."

Ynna knew better than to trust her but felt that she was sincere.

They walked over to a dilapidated couch where a young man and woman sat watching daytime television on a small screen with protruding wires covered in gnaw marks from rats. Both sets of eyes turned to look at them as they approached.

"The two of you make quite a pair," the boy said, standing and extending a hand to Ynna. He was shorter than she and seemed to want to make up for lack of height with width. He was muscular, a large vascular arm reaching out to her from under a black tank top with the words "sponsored product" stenciled across his chest. He had black hair, shaved on the side and slicked back on top. "I'm Metric," he said, shaking with one hand and sweeping his long, greasy hair back with the other. He hooked a thumb to the girl with similar facial features to him and a spiked purple Mohawk. "There's my sister, Pes."

She gave a slight wave, rattling the bands of costume jewelry on her wrist. She was short and plump with piercings covering her ears, nose, and eyebrows. She looked at Ynna with the same derision that Whitney had.

"There are more of us," Metric informed her, "but we are the most important two."

"He thinks of himself as our leader," Whitney explained with an eye roll.

Metric grinned. "I *am* the leader."

"You just keep telling yourself that," Whitney mocked and shoved him playfully. Ynna understood then why the girl had been threatened by her. Ynna would make it clear, as quickly as she could, that she had no interest in the little strongman.

"I'm Ynna," she told the two of them.

Pes snorted. "With the two of you around, we'll be able to pull jobs on all the men in town."

Ynna tried to hide her grimace. All the rich fathers with their genetically designed children had tried to one-up each other through the outward beauty of their offspring. For her whole life, Ynna had been little more than a prop her father had used to aggrandize himself, and now these kids saw her as little more than a pretty girl, too. She wanted to prove her value as more than that.

"I'm Ynna. Killian said you could use another pair of hands," she said, hoping to change the subject.

It didn't work. "I'm surprised he didn't want your pair of hands," Metric said, obviously pleased with his own joke.

"Gross," Ynna said, trying to play it off, but her displeasure was obvious.

Whitney snorted a laugh. "You've clearly never been very desperate."

Ynna looked at her in shock.

She shrugged, averting her eyes. "Desperate times."

Whitney looked to Metric. "What's on the menu for today?"

Metric smiled as Pes chucked him a bag. He opened it to reveal what appeared to be fine jewelry, though Ynna knew better.

"So, what, we get suckers to buy fake stuff for a marked-up price?" Ynna asked, and they all laughed. She felt her face flush with embarrassment.

"No," Metric said. "Much simpler. While you two try to convince rich tourists to buy the shit for their wives, we pick their pockets. The marks will be too distracted by a nice pair of tits to notice as we snatch the cash chip."

Ynna tried her best not to let her annoyance with the comment show. She would go along with the plan and try to befriend them, but she was determined to come up with her own clever plan—though she had to admit to herself that she had no idea where to begin.

"Why do they carry cash chips?" Ynna asked. Though Killian had paid her with one, most people she knew used digital currency exclusively.

"You really are new to the world," Metric laughed, clapping his hands bemusedly.

Whitney put an assuring hand on Ynna's shoulder. "Most of the tourists we target are off-worlders who get chips when they arrive at port."

"Oh," Ynna said, feeling foolish.

"Killian said you were a looker, so we got you this," Pes interjected and threw a band of white fabric at Ynna that she caught awkwardly.

She flipped it over in her hands. "What am I looking at?"

"A top," Whitney chuckled, and Ynna's eyes darted from the fabric to the girl. "Trust me. It'll do the trick."

Of that, Ynna had no doubt. The fabric was light and pale and would be less than she had worn to the beach club on a sweltering day. For the first time since meeting with them, Ynna doubted if she could work with them. "Is there someplace I can change?" she whispered to Whitney.

"Here isn't good enough for you, milady?" Pes snarled. Ynna felt her face burn with rage and humiliation. She considered just telling them to fuck off and go back to her room to finish out the school day. That thought, the idea of sitting in the cramped space, suffering through another lecture, fortified her resolve.

"It's no big deal," Whitney assured her, pulling off her vest to expose the slight bra she wore. "We'll end the day with some cash."

"Fine," Ynna said, determined. She pulled her shirt off with trembling hands and folded it before realizing there was no good place to set it down and simply throwing it on top of a broken box that served as a table. She ignored the eyes on her as she pulled the band over her head and onto her chest. She tried not to pay attention to how little cover it provided as she pulled her bra off from under it.

Metric was beaming, Whitney was looking on her with a surprising face of support, and Pes was staring daggers. She adjusted the top and threw the bra to join her shirt, looking down to see the clear outline of her breasts and nipples showing through the fabric. She looked away to keep from running out the door in shame. She had never worn anything like this and couldn't believe that she was now.

"They definitely won't see us coming," Metric said, almost bursting.

Whitney turned and whispered. "I honestly thought you would run the second you saw that."

"I wanted to," Ynna admitted. She didn't know why she felt comfortable saying that to the girl she had just met, but at that moment, she just needed someone.

"You're doing great," Whitney told her softly. Ynna wondered why she was being so kind all of a sudden but was grateful for it.

"What now?" Ynna asked, trying to sound confident and failing.

"Now we go shopping," Whitney said.

CHAPTER 5

The shopping district by the port was abuzz with activity. People were moving from storefronts to stalls to purchase goods they could not get anywhere but here. Where the people of earth used cybernetic bioaugments to compete with robots for jobs, the off-worlders had used bioengineered rapid evolution to survive on distant planets. Skin of every color, plate calluses, gills, massive eyes, and many other adaptations that changed the human form could be found all around them.

Ynna—having only ever met businesspeople from other planets—was shocked to see how different people could be.

"Crazy, right?" Whitney asked, following Ynna's wide eyes.

"It is," she said, unable to say much more. Metric and Pes had run off to get into position, leaving the two girls to walk the streets and look for a potential victim.

"Want a quick pick-me-up before we get into this?" Whitney asked, gesturing to a shady man in a trench coat standing at the end of an alley.

Ynna couldn't help herself. "Why are you being so nice?"

Whitney stopped walking and turned with a smile. "What?"

"You were so cold this morning, and now you're being all

43

kind, and it's weird," Ynna stated more bluntly than she had ever said anything.

Whitney's smile grew wider. "You. Well, it's just. Killian said you were smart, and then I saw you, and you're also pretty, and I was annoyed. But then when I saw how nervous and over-whelmed you were, I don't know. You reminded me—well, you reminded me of me."

"Oh," Ynna said.

"Yeah," Whitney nearly whispered. "And I didn't have anyone to help me when I started, and I wanted to help you, you know?"

"That's nice," Ynna said, surprised by the answer. "Thank you."

"No problem," Whitney said. "Still wish you were ugly, though."

"Sorry," Ynna chuckled. She felt relieved and happy she had asked. While she hated the outfit they had picked for her, the warm sun of the day felt nice on her skin, and she took just a moment to breathe in deeply before they got to work.

"Whatever," Whitney said in a genial tone. "It'll get us paid, right?"

"Right," Ynna agreed and pointed to the alley. "Now, let's go talk to your sketchy-ass friend."

Whitney grinned and grabbed Ynna's hand, dragging her over to the massive man in the alley.

"Hey, Whit," he said, sounding out of breath though he was just standing there immobile.

"Hey, Tubb," she said.

"Little 'eng for me and a swig for my new friend," she said.

"I got you," he said, producing a nanovial with microinjector and handing it over. She pressed the tip to her arm, and it made a dull popping sound before the liquid entered her body.

"Ooh, boy," she said as a wave of vibration moved from her

feet to her head. She dropped the vial and stamped on it like a cigarette butt. The big man nodded approvingly and pulled a flask from his coat, which he handed to Ynna.

She tried not to think how many mouths had been on the flask as she unscrewed the top, the metal catching on a thin layer of gunk. Hesitantly, she moved it to her lips.

"Woah, woah, woah," Tubb said. "What kind of place you think this is?"

He pulled a small paper cup from another pocket and handed it over. The cup was comically tiny in his massive hand.

"Thanks," Ynna said as she poured herself a shot of whatever this was. It smelled like rubbing alcohol. Taking a sip, she was shocked that it actually didn't taste as bad as it smelled. It was a pleasant surprise.

Whitney looked at her, eyes narrowed and focused.

"Ready to learn a thing?" she asked excitedly.

Ynna smiled. "Yes. Yes, I am."

As they stepped into the street, assessing their prey, Whitney explained, "We want someone confused. Distracted. In over their head here. Someone like—like that."

She pointed to a blue-skinned man with a full, skintight bodysuit and clear plastic dome over his head attached by a hose to a water pack. He left steaming footprints on the ground as he walked the street, looking nervous and overwhelmed.

"Excuse me, sir. Are you looking for something for your wife, perhaps?" Whitney asked as she bound into the space in front of him. Behind auto-adjusting light lenses, his massive eyes went wide with surprise before scanning the two girls the way a dog looks at a food dish set before it.

"Uh, um, yes," he said, the words spraying the water seeping from his headgear.

"Great!" Whitney said with a charming energy Ynna had never seen from her before. "We have just the thing for you!"

She opened the bag and produced a necklace with a green gem hanging from the bottom. "This is jade and gold, two substances unique to earth and something your better half is sure to love."

She kept talking, never giving him even a moment to reply.

As she spoke, Metric rounded a corner casually. Ynna had expected him to skulk out and creep over to steal the money, but he simply strode down the street like any of the other shoppers. As though he was checking out some electronics at a nearby window, he passed behind the blue man and entered a shop.

It all happened so fast that Ynna wasn't even sure if it *had* happened. She couldn't believe how easy it all was. Being a part of it made her nervous, though, and she was grateful for the drink, knowing her hands would be trembling without it. She worked hard to keep her eyes from darting around nervously, looking for Carcer officers.

"So, are you interested?" Whitney finished her pitch with a question.

"Yes, um, well, maybe," he sputtered, seeming confused by the question. "How much?"

"That's the best part, it'll only cost you one hundred thousand," Whitney said, and the man's mouth fell open.

"Oh, no, no. Too much, too much," he said, raising his hands and shifting uncomfortably.

"Alright, no worries, maybe next time," Whitney beamed and nearly skipped away.

"Holy shit," Ynna said when they had moved far enough away.

"Pretty cool, right?" Whitney asked excitedly, a broad grin on her face.

Ynna nodded. "Yes, it happened so fast."

"When you pick the right target, it does," Whitney said, obviously proud of herself.

"What if he had been willing to pay the unreasonable amount?" Ynna asked.

"I just keep jacking the price 'til they back off," she explained.

"Has it ever failed?" Ynna asked.

"Sure, once, but when he realized his money was gone, I made a break for it," Whitney said, looking down and shifting her leg.

"And do they ever get Carcer involved?" Ynna asked nervously.

Whitney laughed. "That's the beauty of it! Most off-worlders have free, governmental police and are in for a rude awakening when they realize they don't have the money to pay Carcer to get their money back! They could take out a loan, but most tourists just here for a weekend don't want to pay the interest. Works like a charm."

Ynna realized then that she had not understood Carcer properly. As a rich kid, the officers had mostly seemed like their protectorate, but for those without money, there could be no justice.

"Is what we are doing wrong?" Ynna asked before adding, "philosophically, I mean."

Whitney stopped for a moment and looked at her. "Yeah, I mean, kinda."

"Oh," Ynna said, not thrilled about the answer. She had hoped to have her guilt assuaged, but now she felt uncomfortable.

Whitney noticed. "But what you have to understand is that we have nothing, and these people," she gestured to the shoppers with armloads of bags. "They have enough money to spend a whole day buying shit. And what's more, many of them can afford a flight to a different fucking planet. If they have that kind of money, they really aren't going to miss what we snatch."

The justification was weak, but it was enough to satisfy Ynna.

THE REST of the day went smoothly. They picked a few more pockets. Whitney even gave Ynna a chance to try her hand at distraction. Ynna sounded awkward and uncomfortable in her own ears, sputtering, and stuttering.

"I—I think she would like this," she forced, producing a ring with a trembling hand.

"Ooh, that's nice," the mark said, eyeing it as Pes strode over behind him. Remembering what Whitney had taught her, Ynna made sure to keep her eyes firmly on the target though she couldn't help but want to watch the thieving unfold. Her heart thrummed, and it took all her strength not to blow their cover.

"Yes, it's a rare gym. I'm so sorry, *gem* that you can only get here," she said, trying to laugh off her mistake.

"It's pretty, like you," the mark said, and Ynna understood why they had forced her into the attire. It almost didn't matter what she said so long as the men had something to gawk at. As gross as it felt, she did enjoy the power it gave her over the foolish men who were too preoccupied with her body to notice the world around them.

She told him the exorbitant price, and like the rest, he waved the girls off.

As they strode away, Ynna caught a glimpse of something out of the corner of her eye and threw Whitney into a narrow alley, pressing her against the wall.

Whitney laughed. "I don't really play this way," she joked, clearly able to see the nerves in Ynna's action.

"No, it's not, it's—" Ynna said, and Whitney laughed again.

"I got that," she said, craning her neck to follow Ynna's gaze. "See someone you know?"

Ynna nodded vigorously. They watched as a girl in the telltale academy uniform flounced next to her mother and a drudge carrying shopping bags.

"You were one of them?" Whitney asked in astonishment. "You really *have* fallen far."

At that moment, Ynna could not have agreed more. She had spent the day robbing people for less than she used to spend on a night out. What struck Ynna as strange was that while she was embarrassed and didn't want her classmate to see her, she didn't envy the girl's life. She had been just like that so recently—an impatient little girl dogging her mother's steps through shops. Now, dressed uncomfortably and stealing from people, she felt independent for the first time.

"Want to call it a day?" Whitney asked, kindness in her voice.

Ynna smiled, knowing she still had things to do. "Yes, please."

CHAPTER 6

The apartment was still empty when Ynna returned, gripping the cash chip containing her portion of the takings. She had been surprised after seeing how little her cut was, compared to how large Killian's was, but she was pleased to have made money for the first time in her life.

She jammed the chip in a pile of clothes she was sure no one would rummage through. Gato purred loudly as she approached, checking that she had completed her schooling. A broad grin crossed her lips as she saw the green checkmark. She changed quickly and nearly bound out the door for her self-defense class, as it was the one part of her forced education that she enjoyed.

She had felt her body getting stronger as the classes progressed, and she enjoyed feeling less weak and timid as she learned. After a long day of growing more independent, she welcomed the opportunity to continue in that direction.

SWEATY AND TIRED AFTER CLASS, she walked the few short blocks back to the apartment with confidence, feeling as if today was the first day of her life. The streets were well lit with floodlights bolted to buildings, open flames, and the neon signs that suggested something seedy within the crumbling walls. As she walked past a costume shop, she stopped to stare at the holoprojected model wearing an Ancient Roman military costume. Her eyes grew wide as the man posed and shifted positions. As she looked at the leather skirt, cut into pointed strips, she smiled.

Her father had determined her look for her whole life. Now, free of him, she could make a fashion all her own. She raced back to the apartment, flinging open the crappy door with a bang she worried would wake Marco. When she heard no stirring, she darted into her room and rummaged through all the old stuff they had come with. She quickly found what she was looking for—the old pleated skirt from her school. It used to tell the world she was a spoiled rich girl, and now she would wear it with pride, a reminder that she was no longer that person.

She reached over to the sewing kit her mother had bought to hem her uniforms and got to work.

THE NEXT SEVERAL months flew by in a blur. Ynna spent her days with Whitney and the crew, and her nights learning to fight to defend herself. She got better at both, realizing that she was a good student when she was interested. She still wanted to come up with a scheme all her own to help her friends make money, but she enjoyed learning the ploys and cons they used. Metric began to teach her to hide in plain sight and how to make herself invisible in a crowd or how to draw attention as a diversion.

She grew to like not only the lessons but the crew as well. For the first time, she felt that she had real friends, though Pes never seemed to warm to her and always seemed guarded when Ynna was around.

She was moving up in her defense class, too. She was becoming more skilled, more quickly than even some students who had started long before her. Her instructor took great pride in her progress and worked her harder than anyone else in the class. She grew to love the praise and didn't mind that she was dead tired, soaked in sweat, and covered in bruises when she finally made her way home at night.

As she approached the apartment one evening, she was surprised to see the light on in the window that overlooked the street.

She walked up the stairs cautiously and was shocked to find Hector on the couch, nursing a beer and watching the evening news. He turned slowly to look at her as she entered the room.

"I know you are not classing," he said, not as an accusation as much as an observation.

"Oh, no. I—" Ynna began to protest, but Hector clicked his tongue and patted the couch next to him. She sat, the cold, damp perspiration sending a chill down her spine.

"Please do not deny. Killian is bad actor," he explained. His face was unreadable, and his voice flat.

"I'm sorry," Ynna said, letting her head drop.

"Disingenuous does not suit you," Hector said, muting the screen and turning to face her.

Ynna pouted. "I'm growing and enjoying it," she justified.

"That's good, but not what your mother wants," he said, and again, it sounded more like a simple statement of truth.

Ynna found herself bothered that she couldn't read the situation. With so many others, she felt as if she knew exactly how to play them, how to give them what they needed so she could get what she wanted. Right now, with Hector, she didn't know what to say. He was a cipher, taking in her words and giving her little.

"It is a hard thing," he told her. "Deciding how to spend one's time. Your mother, she want what is best. She may not know what that is."

The corner of Ynna's mouth turned up slightly. "Do you?" she asked, before clarifying, "know what's best for me?"

He smiled for the first time. It was only a hint, but Ynna caught it. "For you? I don't presume such things. For Marco, yes, but for you, no. I think your mother no sees what makes you strong."

Ynna noted that his accent was much more pronounced as he spoke so candidly. She assumed it was also not his first beer. "Why do you think that is?" she asked, genuinely curious.

He wrapped his free hand around the back of his neck, thinking a moment. "Your mother sees what is in front of her. She plans for future, but maybe not for long future. She has been this way, always."

Ynna saw her opening. "How long have you known her?"

He nodded, accepting that he was going to give in and tell her. "Long time. We grew up as one. She was as mi hermana— my sister," he said, clasping his hands, the beer slushing softly. "Both of us want more. We find more in different ways," he unhooked his fingers and spread his arms wide. "She marry rich, I do business. We both find what we need."

Ynna had figured that they were old friends. It was all that had made sense. Karen had slid so easily into the life here that Ynna knew it couldn't be her first time. She wanted to ask more questions, press him for information, but let the silence hang.

"She lose everything," he continued. "She come home. She go back to work. This life, she knows. For you, I think she has no plan. She sends you to school because it makes sense. But beyond such—" He shrugged.

"And what do you think?" she asked.

"You strong. Smart. Determined. But purposeless," he said, and it didn't land as an insult, she actually agreed. She had been so focused on what was right in front of her and trying to succeed and fit in that she hadn't stopped a moment to consider what she wanted from her life.

"For you, I cannot answer. You must answer for yourself," he put plainly, and her heart sank a little. She knew he was right but had hoped he would make it easy and tell her something. Anything, really.

"You going to tell my mom about school?" she asked nervously, though she suspected the answer. She did not want to give up her days with her new friends, and could not imagine going back to sitting in the stuffy apartment all day, bored out of her skull in a digital classroom.

He smiled kindly. "No, but you should."

That answer was almost worse. Ynna didn't want to have to tell her mother that she had given up her education. She knew Karen wouldn't understand.

"You're right," she admitted despite herself.

"I usually am," he said, holding up his beer in salute to himself before taking another sip.

"Want another?" she asked, standing and making her way toward the fridge.

He nodded, and she grabbed two before rejoining him on the couch. His point was made, so he turned the volume back up on the screen, and they drank in silence until she dragged herself to bed.

IT WAS dark when an ear-splitting boom awakened her. The apartment shook with the sound, and Ynna instinctively reached over to check if her mother was next to her.

She was not.

Ynna popped up and dashed to the door, cracking it slightly as she heard shouting voices fill the apartment. Armed people were entering through the smoking frame of the door with weapons drawn. Beams of light moved in every direction from the front of the guns.

Light blinded her as a shape moved in her direction.

"On the ground!" an authoritative voice ordered, and she dropped to her knees instinctively. The shape checked a screen on its wrist as it pointed a gun in her face.

"Nothing on the girl," the voice said to the others.

As more lights moved toward Hector's room, she heard a loud crack and the lights moved wildly as one of the shapes fell to the ground.

"In here!" another barked, and the lights converged on Hector's room.

As her eyes adjusted, Ynna saw the scorpion pincer logo of Carcer Corp on the black armor of the intruders. She heard Hector call out before the wall that connected the rooms shook with a thump.

Through the beam of light in her face, she could just make out Hector's form as he was dragged from the room.

Marco had never come home, and Ynna questioned if Hector had known what was coming.

She blinked hard and saw him being dragged out of the room by two large men. He had a gash across his forehead and blood, which looked black in the darkness, poured down his face.

"The apartment is paid," he rasped to her. "You stay. Marco with his abuela. Tell your mom I—" His words were cut short by the butt of a rifle. Ynna felt her whole body tighten at the sound of the crack. He didn't need to finish the sentence, though. She knew. She had known since the moment they walked into the apartment. Her mother had looked on him in a way that Ynna had never seen before, and he doted on the two of them like a little boy excited to carry a girl's books to class.

Hector and Karen were a love story that would never be.

His body was limp, and he spoke no more as the intruders dragged him from the room, followed by the body of the one Carcer officer Hector had shot.

When the room was all but empty, the voice from behind the light said to Ynna, "Keep your nose clean, and we won't be back for you."

He spun and disappeared into the blackness.

Ynna sat on the floor, trembling and sobbing.

As her eyes adjusted again, she stared at the dark stains on the floor, illuminated by small LED lights of the various devices around the house. She took short, shallow breaths, wishing she had done something. She had let them take him without a fight. In the future, she would come to understand that there was nothing she could have done, but at that moment, she hated herself for her inaction. She thought about how she could have disarmed the officer who put the gun too close to her face and use his weapon to fight off the others. She thought about how she could have tried to stall them, keep them occupied, and bought him time to escape.

She wondered again if he had known. He had come home early, talked with her, and drank. He had kept Marco out of the house. It was all too unusual to be a coincidence. It also would explain why he had chosen this night to have their heart to heart.

Her mind swam with self-admonishments and questions.

No one came to the apartment. No one came to look. Carcer officers kicking down a door and the sound of gunshots was hardly something people even got out of bed for in this neighborhood.

So, Ynna just sat, staring at the blood in the darkness.

. . .

She was jolted back into consciousness by the sound of a woman's scream. She looked around in confusion and saw the light of early day, and the apartment smeared with crimson stains.

Her mother rushed over and embraced Ynna, who still sat on the floor in the doorway to her room.

"Honey, are you alright?" Karen asked, taking her daughter's face in her hands. Ynna noted how rough her mother's palms felt. They were calloused and worn and so different from how they had been before. "What happened?" Karen asked quietly.

"I—I couldn't stop them," Ynna said, still blaming herself.

"Oh. Oh, honey," her mother soothed. "It wasn't your fault. None of this is your fault."

Ynna could hear the heartbreak in Karen's words.

"What happened? Where's Hector?" she asked, and Ynna was able to put her own feelings aside a moment and notice how terrified and frantic her mom was.

Ynna took a deep breath, feeling as if it were the first one in a long time. "He was taken."

Karen's eyes went wide. "Taken? By whom?"

"Carcer," Ynna told her solemnly.

Karen sank to the floor, puddling into Ynna. "Oh," she said.

They were silent for a long time.

"Those assholes!" Karen finally blurted. It was the most genuine moment Ynna had ever experienced with her mother.

"Yeah," Ynna agreed, unable to shake from her mind the image of Hector being dragged from the apartment.

"You know they charge local businesses for protection? Salesmen come in and ask a ridiculous fee to put a Carcer logo in the window. Then they make veiled threats about how unprotected a business is without them," Karen hissed venomously. "So, you know what most people do?"

Ynna thought about it a moment. "Put fake logos in the windows?"

Karen tapped her finger to her nose.

Ynna was happy to take her mind off the blood-stained floor and talk. "You know," she began, "some off-world communities have government police forces."

Karen snorted a laugh. "Can you imagine anything worse? I think the only thing more corrupt than a private police force would be one run by the Mayor's Office."

Ynna nodded though she didn't really agree. In talking with Metric about the societies on other planets, she had come to like the idea of a civic force whose job it was to keep the citizenry safe.

They fell silent once more.

"You want me to stay with you today? I'm supposed to head back in a few hours, and we will need to get this place cleaned up, and you should get out of the house," Karen offered. She was visibly shaken, and Ynna could see her mother was struggling, too. Both of them had been through so much, and Karen was going to be very unhappy for a very long time with Hector gone. Ynna thought that the best thing for both of them would be to go about their routines. Together, they would spend the day thinking about how sad they were and how bad things would be now. Apart, Ynna hoped they could both keep themselves distracted.

"No, we need the money you can earn today," she told her mother. It was not lost on her that Karen seemed to already know that they could keep the apartment. "You go to work, and I'll go down the street to the drudge rental and hire one to clean up."

"Oh," Karen said, surprised at the offer. "Are you sure? I notice you have started to dress your own way. Seriously, I could take the day, and we could have a little shop, like in the old days."

Ynna smiled at the sweetness of the suggestion. "I'll be okay, mom. Plus, it was a shopping trip that got us into this in the first place."

Karen rolled her eyes. "No matter how many times I tell you this isn't your fault?"

"No matter how many times," Ynna agreed. She watched her mother's eyes drift back to the stain. "Mom," Ynna said to get her attention. "You going to be okay?"

Karen did not answer for a long moment.

"Yes," she said unconvincingly, before adding, "I think so."

"You'll let me know if you need anything, or even if you just need to talk?" Ynna asked quietly.

"Yes, honey. Thank you," Karen said, the light of day now beginning to fill the room. "Should we shut this door and lay down?"

"Yes, please," Ynna said, pushing the door closed with her foot. They both moved toward the bed and collapsed.

CHAPTER 7

Ynna's whole body ached when she awoke. The combination of her workout and the mental strain of the night before made her body feel leaden. She vaguely remembered her mom waking her up when she left for work, but it was little more than a wisp of memory now.

She stood slowly and made her way to the door, discovering that Karen had draped a blanket over the bloodstains, hints of brown staining through the fabric to the surface. She shuddered.

The apartment felt empty, and Gato was nowhere to be found. She poured yesterday's coffee into a cup and gulped it down quickly before remembering Hector's beers. She opened one and took it with her to the shower.

ONCE SHE WAS clean and dressed, she felt like a new woman.

She tried to put the events of the previous night out of her head as she stepped on the door that had been blasted off its hinges. She awkwardly pulled it up and leaned it on the frame, knowing it would do nothing to stop someone if they chose to break in.

She plodded down the street toward the drudge rental, looking the whole time at the Carcer emblems taped and hung in the store windows and doors. Thinking about what her mother had said, she had an idea right on the tip of her brain that she could not quite grab.

Ynna entered Mama's Discount Drudge Rentals to find a girl not much older than Marco sitting on a stool behind the counter, swinging her legs as she watched a cartoon on a screen set into the counter. The walls of the shop were lined with dilapidated humanoid robots under pictures in dusty frames of the jobs they could complete.

"Greetings, ma'am," the girl said, looking up and shooting Ynna a wide smile.

"You mama?" Ynna joked, and the girl snickered, covering her mouth with a tiny hand.

"No, ma'am," she chuckled. "Mama's not even my mom. She's my grandma."

"Ah, and you run the shop for her?" Ynna asked, surprised that the kid would be left alone in this neighborhood.

"Just while mom's on lunch," the girl explained.

"I see," Ynna said, stroking her chin in mock intense thought. "You don't go to school?"

"School's lame," the girl answered, cocking her head and putting on a pout.

Ynna winked. "On that, we agree."

"Something I can help you with," the girl's tone became businesslike.

"Oh," Ynna said, slightly surprised by the shift. "Yes, please. I need a drudge, probably only an hour's work for a door repair and cleanup."

The girl smiled. "No problem, but blood stains are extra."

Ynna smirked. "What makes you think there are bloodstains?"

The girl's face fell flat. "There's always bloodstains. You think I'm some kind of idiot?"

"No. No, I do not," Ynna said. She followed it up with, "Actually, you seem rather savvy."

The girl beamed. "Yep, I'm pretty great." She kicked her legs excitedly. "Just synch your account with the screen, and we'll charge you after."

"I was hoping to pay with a cash chip," Ynna told her, producing the chip from a pocket.

The girl's face was utter shock. "A cash chip? What are you, like, a hundred?"

Ynna laughed and pressed her hands to her heart in mock offense. "You wound me, madam."

The girl laughed, too. "Hand over the chip, old-timer," she said, extending a palm and pressing the chip against a reader on the counter.

She handed the chip back and tried to cover her amusement as she said, "We also have ones that can change your adult diapers."

Ynna guffawed.

"I'm funny, too," the girl said, obviously pleased with herself.

"Well, it was nice to meet you," Ynna said, extending a hand expectantly.

"Doro," the girl said.

"Nice to meet you, Doro. I'm Ynna. I hope our paths cross again," she said, shaking the girl's hand.

Doro chuckled. "Path? What's that, like, some old-time street?"

Ynna smiled. "Not your best joke."

Doro huffed but smiled, too.

She left the shop having completely put the night before

from her mind. She was impressed with the girl. At such a young age, she seemed smarter and more capable than Ynna felt. She had been afforded all the advantages of life but was completely ill-equipped for the real world. Yet here was this girl, much younger and much more prepared.

WHEN SHE ARRIVED at The Press, she was not surprised to find that her friends were already out for the day. Feeling lost and lonely, she wandered aimlessly. She considered eating something, but her body rejected the idea.

A street preacher, promoting some religion of old, hollered, "Hear the good news, everyone." He waved a leather-bound book as the denizens of the city tried to avoid eye contact.

Ynna moved to avoid him as well and was faced with another Carcer logo mounted on a suction-cupped hook in a shop window.

Ynna stopped. Her heart raced, and her hands went numb.

She had an idea.

She ran over to a comm booth and stepped in, quickly searching the database and placing the call. The screen displayed her own face as it rang.

"Hello?" the plump, confused face said.

"Rose," Ynna said. "Hi."

"Ynna?" Rose said, obviously not expecting to see her. "How are you? Oh, gosh, I heard your Dad threw you out. We miss you at school. How are you? Are you okay?"

The concern sounded genuine. Guilt filled Ynna as she realized the girl they had played was more concerned about her than any of her supposed friends. "I'm okay," she said. "I was hoping you could help me with something."

"Of course, anything! You know, when you dropped off, I

asked the girls how I could reach out, but all of them said they didn't know how to contact you," Rose told her.

Ynna scowled. "Of course, they did."

"I just wanted to reach out to tell you I was here for you if you needed anything," she explained.

Ynna could hardly stand the undeserved kindness.

"Thank you, that's really sweet," she said.

"The least I could do," Rose offered.

Ynna chuckled a cold, hard laugh. "Well, the least you could do is nothing. It's what everyone else did. But it's nice you thought of me. Would you have time to meet up?"

"That'd be great!" Rose said excitedly. "You want to swing by the apartment? Mom's at work so we would have the place to ourselves."

"That'd be perfect," Ynna agreed, and the address appeared on the screen.

Ynna dedicated it to memory. "I'll leave now. It will be a bit."

"No worries. I'm here, and I'll tell the guards to let you in," Rose said.

"See you soonish," Ynna said, ending the transmission.

She headed quickly for the cab pad, choosing to fly rather than take the time with a ground vehicle. When she entered the address and saw the price, she questioned her decision but wanted to get her plan in motion, knowing that if she were successful, they would all be earning enough to easily refill their coffers.

Nervous anticipation and excitement coursed through her as the cab lifted, leaving the destitute part of the city for the sparkling downtown skyrises. She was thrilled that she had come up with a proper plan, that she would be able to potentially leave the revealing outfits and low-level cons behind her.

The cab moved quickly, the programmed traffic flowing easily through the skies.

As the glinting city center moved toward her, she realized how disconnected she now felt from the place she had called home her whole life. All the rich people with their lavish lives felt as far to her as the off-world colonies.

Flashing screens and projected ads filled her vision as they approached the tower with a massive Carcer logo spinning on top. Even seeing it made her skin crawl, and she wanted more than anything to hurt that company the way it had damaged her. It didn't matter to her that this building was just a housing complex for employees and their families; the very sight of the logo made her sick.

"A security clearance is required to land at this address," a computerized voice said through the speaker in the back of the cab.

"Ynna," she intoned.

"Marina Anne Hawkins is cleared as a guest," the cab told her. She grimaced at the sound of her full name.

The cab set down. Ynna stepped out, and cameras turned to follow her. An electronic scanner ran over the length of her body to check for weapons while another ran imaging on her face. The scanners shut off, and a green light flashed on an elevator set into the roof.

As she stepped in, she saw that there were no buttons, and she looked to the bulb with a camera mounted on the ceiling of the elevator.

"Miss Hawkins, you are cleared to enter room 4390 only. Any diversion from this will be seen as a violation of the visitor code of conduct, and you will be escorted from the premises," a woman's voice boomed in the small space.

The doors closed, and the elevator plummeted at a sickening speed before lurching to a stop on the fourth floor. A bell rang, the doors opened, and she stepped out, trying to get her bearings. A digital display pointed her in the direction of the apartment. As she walked, the walls displayed arrows that were clearly meant to lead her in the correct direction.

As she made her way down the fluorescent-lit, white hallway, she heard a voice call out, "Ynna!"

She looked up from the wall just in time to see Rose rushing toward her. She enveloped Ynna in a warm embrace. Ynna lifted her hands awkwardly to return the hug.

Rose was heavy, a head shorter than her, and dressed in a loose-fitting gray sweatsuit. She had narrow eyes and pale skin with her black hair.

"It's good to see you," Ynna said, letting her arms fall. It was a moment before Rose released her, looking up and smiling.

"You look great, love the new look," she said, rubbing Ynna's hair between her thumb and forefinger.

Ynna had started coloring her hair pink, and though the roots would show, she liked the way it looked, too. She was saving to have her hair microdyed, but that would have to wait.

"And the skirt," Rose continued to gush. "You turned our stupid uniform into some badass-bitch version of Julius Caesar!"

Ynna smiled. When Whitney and the gang had seen her new look, they liked it but never seemed to get what she was going for.

She remembered why she had liked Rose. While the other girls in her old clique had found the girl cloying and obnoxious, Ynna had always thought she was pure and nice.

"Thanks," Ynna said, trying not to let her pleasure with the compliment show too much.

"Come in, come in," Rose said, ushering her into the massive apartment. Ynna looked around the room, shocked that she used to live this way, too.

The room was massive and open with one entire wall made of glass, looking out onto the city. An island bar flanked one side with a kitchen behind and looked into the living space with a pristine leather couch—worth more than the entire building where Ynna currently lived—facing a wallscreen. Ynna figured the couch had never been sat on, and the screen never turned on.

Artistic photographs of scorpions adorned the walls, hung in ornate frames. Ynna chuckled to herself, wondering if every apartment in the complex had the same Carcer interior designer.

"Something to drink?" Rose offered. "We've got soda, juice, or actual water if you want."

"Got any beers?" Ynna asked without thinking.

Rose's eyes went wide. "Wow, a few months on the mean streets, and what are you some kind of alcoholic?"

"I'm some kind of something," Ynna said with a little laugh.

"That tap there on the fridge has wine if you want?" she said, hurrying over to get a glass from a cabinet.

Ynna laughed at the absurdity of it all. "That'll do."

Rose handed her a glass.

"You're not going to have one?" Ynna asked.

Rose's face registered a new surprise. "I mean, I never have."

"Live a little," Ynna said and handed the glass back to her before going to fetch her own. She filled it nearly to the brim and took a sip. The sweet liquid coated her tongue, and she moaned. "Fuuuuck, that's good."

Rose giggled and took a sip herself. "Yeah," she agreed and then dropped her head sheepishly.

"So, what's up? I mean, I'm glad to see you and all, but I don't think you stopped by just for a taste of the high life."

"You're right," Ynna said and took another swig. "Can we go to your room?" As the words left her mouth, she hated that spending so much time with Killian made her worried that it sounded suggestive.

Rose didn't read it that way. "Sure."

Ynna's mouth fell open as she entered the room. She had expected it to be furnished like that of a child, but instead, all the walls were screens, and there was a bed and a desk, and nothing else. Three of the walls were set to show images of the inside of the Egypt section of a museum, and she had to work hard to tell her mind that she could not just stride down the halls to look at the busts and artifacts. The wall that the desk was pressed against was set to an aerial shot of Giza.

"You like?" Rose asked timidly, and Ynna wondered if she had ever had anyone over to her place before.

"It's lovely. I'm just—" Ynna stopped herself.

"What?" Rose asked nervously.

"I don't know. I guess I just figured you for a physical book kind of person," Ynna admitted.

"Oh," Rose said with a smile. She tapped her palm, and one of the walls opened to reveal a shelving unit full of books and what Ynna assumed were actual Egyptian artifacts.

"There it is!" Ynna exclaimed with pride, rushing over to appraise the shelf.

Rose seemed thrilled that she was impressed, and they stood in silence a moment before Ynna turned to her.

"So, I'm going to say something, and you may not like it," Ynna said.

Rose's face dropped. "Yeah?"

"Carcer is not a good company," Ynna said, hoping the girl wouldn't throw her out of the apartment on the spot.

Rose let out a loud, deep laugh. "Oh, gosh! I thought you were going to say something mean or play some trick on me."

Ynna's heart broke at the comment, wondering how many times the girl had been burned.

"No kidding, Carcer is all kinds of evil," Rose said. "Lots of people in this place would be aghast to hear me say it, but they have blinders on."

Ynna breathed a sigh of relief. "So, you wouldn't mind hacking their system?"

Rose shifted uncomfortably. "I mean, I guess. I just can't be caught, or I'll be sharing a room with you," she said, worrying her hands. "Or worse."

"You getting caught is the last thing I want, too," Ynna assured her. "If it looks like you can't break it, just back out."

"Okay," Rose said, swiveling in her chair toward the wall that turned into multiple windows of lines of code. "What are we looking for?"

Ynna's guilt was renewed at Rose's eagerness to please despite the risk. She knew she was putting an innocent girl in danger for this. She had told Rose to keep herself safe, but she really wanted the information. Ynna gritted her teeth, resolved to see this through.

"There should be a database somewhere in there of stores who do and don't pay protection to the company," Ynna explained.

"Sure," Rose said, tapping at a digital keyboard in the desk. "What do you want this for?"

"Would it offend you if I said that for your sake, it's better that you don't know?" Ynna asked, hoping the implication was enough to back her off.

Rose snorted. "I'm all about plausible deniability."

"Good," Ynna said, leaning on the desk to watch what Rose was doing. "Can you explain to me what you are doing as you are doing it? I kinda want to learn this stuff."

"Sure!" Rose said, sounding thrilled at the prospect of imparting some knowledge.

She talked Ynna through the process of hacking the system, and Ynna came to understand that she would need to study a lot more to actually understand this. Despite that, she listened with rapt attention, trying to soak it all in.

"Wow," Rose said, surprised.

"What?" Ynna asked.

"This was super easy," Rose explained. "It's almost as if they want someone to be able to find this."

Ynna smirked. "Assholes."

"What?" Rose said, turning to Ynna.

"They probably *do* want someone to be able to find this," Ynna said in disgust.

"Why?" Rose asked, and Ynna felt like she was playing at naïve. "What are you planning to do?"

Ynna let her face fall flat. "As I said."

"Better I don't know," Rose repeated, but Ynna knew she was on to the plan. "You want all of it or some particular districts?"

"I'll never be able to make heads or tails of all of it. Just Redwood Point would be fine."

"Oh my," Rose said. "*That's* where you're staying?"

Ynna chuckled. "Don't believe everything you hear. The streets below *this* tower are just as dangerous. People just fear the unknown."

"If you say so." Rose sounded unconvinced. "It's so safe that you've doubled in muscle mass, dress like you want to kick someone's ass, and are covered in bruises?"

Ynna was taken aback by the comment at first but, looking down at herself, had to admit the truth in Rose's words. "Alright, maybe it's a little less safe."

"There you go," Rose said smugly. "Alright, you got something I can transfer this intel to?"

Ynna looked at the ground.

"Oh," Rose said. "I didn't mean anything by it. You want a pair of my old lenscreens? I can easily transfer ownership and teach you how to use them."

Ynna rotated a foot on one toe. She didn't want handouts, didn't want to have to accept further kindness from someone she had so mistreated, but knew she had no choice. Her father had disabled her smart devices the moment they had walked through the door, and they hadn't needed them since moving. "Sure," Ynna accepted, but her shame coated the word.

"Ynna," Rose said in a kind voice, swiveling to face her and taking another sip of the wine. "Look, I know you are proud, and you notice I haven't asked about what happened, but it's okay to take help when you need it.

"I was in a really dark place when you and the girls started talking to me. I'm not an idiot, and I knew what you wanted, but I needed friends then even if they were fake. I didn't even care when you dropped me because being seen with you guys for a week gave me enough cachet to start my own little band of losers."

Ynna felt horrible about her actions despite how Rose turned them to her advantage. She knew that Rose's words did not absolve her, and she felt all the more guilty for just showing up when she needed something. She had been annoyed (though not surprised) that none of her friends had reached out to her, but she hadn't reached out to anyone, either. She looked up at Rose, her eyes burning, "I'm really sorry."

"I know," Rose said, putting a comforting hand on her shoulder. "I always knew. The little waves and head nods my way were the reason I knew you were different, and the reason I didn't hang up on you the second I saw your face earlier."

"Thanks," Ynna said, her spirits improving slightly.

"So take the lenses and if you need anything else, like money or anything—" she began.

"No," Ynna stopped her.

"What if I insisted," Rose said, and Ynna wondered if the wine was giving her new confidence.

"I'd still say no," Ynna said flatly.

Rose rolled her eyes. "You'd just be taking money from Carcer, and they're evil, remember?"

"No," Ynna insisted. "I'd be taking from you, and you've done enough already. You took a huge risk breaking into the system, even if it was easy. And with the lenses, it's all too much."

"Fine," Rose said, but a sly grin crossed her lips. "Let's set up the lenses, then."

ROSE TOOK her time explaining all the various functions of the lenses and uploaded the Carcer data in such a way that Ynna could look at a shop in her district and know if they paid for protection. They both finished their wine and lazed for a bit on the couch before Ynna realized how late it was getting.

"So, what's your plan after you finish school?" she asked.

"Well," Rose began, excitement obvious in her words, "in the fall, I'll be moving to Tel Aviv."

She said the last part with a clear implication. Ynna beamed. "No! You got in?"

"I did!" Rose squealed, and Ynna wrapped her arms around the girl. The Tel Aviv Academy of Computer Arts was where all the brightest computer minds went to school to learn how to make money for the big companies within the digital worlds. There were many ways in which people could make huge amounts by farming supplies, setting up ads, and crafting materials in the massively popular virtual worlds. The University taught young folks all these skills, but they were known for another thing as well: recruiting and training the world's best hackers.

"I'm so proud of you," Ynna said. "Shit, in a few years, you'll be able to afford a place way nicer than this!"

Rose nodded. "It's not really about the money I'll be able to make, but that won't hurt."

"It definitely won't," Ynna told her.

"I'm just excited to learn some skills that may be able to help me make the world a better place," Rose said, entirely genuine.

Ynna matched her sincerity. "That's great."

"My mom will be home any minute," Rose reminded her, and Ynna stood.

"Thank you," she said, moving to the door. "For everything."

"It's my pleasure, Ynna. And if you ever need anything—" she began.

"I won't," Ynna said.

"How about: if you ever get into a pinch or find a way I can help the world?" she led.

"I'll call you," Ynna finished, and they hugged again.

Years later, when Ynna would watch Rose be gunned down by Carcer officers, she would never tell anyone how deeply it broke her heart. She would play tough and turn the page, but she would never forget what Rose had done for her and what it had meant to have a true friend.

CHAPTER 8

Ynna had to keep herself from breaking into a run as she moved toward The Press the following morning.

The drudge had done an excellent job, and Karen had come home early with food from the restaurant for them to eat. They watched tv together until they both fell asleep. Ynna was happy her mom had taken such an interest in making sure they spent time together after the incident the night before, but she was almost too excited about the prospect of talking to her friends to care.

SHE WAS PANTING when she came upon Whitney.

"I've got it," she said.

Whitney turned in confusion and raised an eyebrow. "Got what?"

"A plan," Ynna wheezed.

"Oh," Whitney said with a curious smile.

"So you can put your tits away, and we can make some real money," Ynna told her.

"I like the sound of that," Whitney said.

Whitney got the attention of Metric and Pes, and they both turned somewhat dubious eyes on Ynna.

"Okay," she began, putting her hand on a pole to steady herself and catch her breath. The ancient wood crumbled at the touch, and Ynna pulled away. "So, you guys know that Carcer offers protection to local businesses to keep people from breaking in?"

"Yeah," Metric said.

"You just figured that out?" Pes put in.

"No, shut up," Ynna snarled playfully. "Let me finish. So, most places don't pay and just put fake signs in the windows to keep from getting robbed."

"Everyone knows that. Most of us hoodlums are pretty good at spotting the fakes," Metric said, smiling to himself.

"Met, if you don't let me finish, I'm going to put you through that fucking wall," Ynna said, gesturing threateningly.

"I'd like to see you try," Metric said under his breath but loud enough to be heard clearly.

"I would, too," Pes added. "I'll put fifty on Ynna."

"Will you guys let her finish?" Whitney screamed, and the two shifted as if her words were a gust of wind.

"Fine, sorry," Pes said.

"Yeah, sorry, Whit," Metric raised his hands defensively.

Whitney made a sweeping motion with her hand. "The floor is yours."

Ynna smiled. "Most people think they can spot the fakes but don't actually act on it because there is a chance Carcer actually protects the place. The risk isn't worth the reward."

"Right," Whitney agreed.

"But I snagged a list," Ynna said, puffing herself up and folding her arms with pride.

"Wait. What?" Metric asked.

"A list of the places Carcer protects?" Whitney looked astonished.

"Yes," Ynna said, a little smug. "And I have intel from their database, so we will know which shops are fronts for dealers and drug runners and the like."

"No. Shit," Whitney said.

"We are gonna be rich," Pes muttered.

The three looked on her with such reverence that Ynna never wanted the moment to end.

"Now, we can rob some bad people and turn a nice little profit for ourselves," she explained, though they had all come to understand that. She just wanted to rub it in.

Whitney looked at her with wide, happy eyes. "This is amazing."

"Yeah, Yn, this will change our lives. How the hell did you do it?" Metric asked, sounding as if he was still in shock.

Ynna smirked and said cryptically, "I know people."

"Yeah, you fucking do," Metric said.

"I guess we have to tell Killian and have him give us some gear," Whitney said. "We will need guns and ammo and masks and stuff."

Ynna's heart sank. She hadn't considered that they would need to bring Killian in on this. She knew Whitney was right. They would not be able to pull jobs in the area without telling him, and they didn't have the supplies to rob drug dealers, but she wasn't happy about having to tell him.

"Any way we can leave the list out of it?" she asked.

The three exchanged nervous glances.

"If he finds out we've been withholding," Metric said implicitly.

Ynna groaned. "Fine."

.   .   .

THEY WERE GIDDY as they entered Killian's shop, and he looked up and smiled. Ynna was grateful his eyes came to rest on Whitney.

"If it isn't my favorite group of hooligans," he said.

"Hey, Kil," Metric said, taking the lead. "We want to start running some harder jobs."

Killian shot them a dubious look. "Do you now?"

"Yes, we need you to kit us out with weapons and armor," Metric said, using a hat-in-hand tone.

Killian stifled a laugh. "You think you're ready for the big leagues?"

"We do," Whitney spoke in a tough voice.

Killian was unimpressed. "It'll take more than shaking that little ass to play with the big boys."

The inherent sexism made Ynna want to spit. She wanted to throw the fact that it was *her* who was making this possible in his face. She felt her face flush with anger, but she held her tongue.

"We've got a leg up," Metric said, trying to diffuse the situation. Whitney looked as bothered as Ynna felt.

"It'll take more than a leg up, kid," Killian made no effort to hide his condescension.

Metric blurted, "We know who pays for Carcer protection."

At that, Killian's face contorted before he could play it cool. "Is that right?"

"Yeah, so we need some gear if we are going to step up our game," Ynna put in, trying to divert the conversation away from the revelation.

Killian was no fool and did not let the subject drop. "How did a group such as yourselves come upon such valuable information?"

"We know people," Whitney parroted Ynna's words.

"Some very well-connected people it seems," Killian said,

eyeing them with new suspicion. "And I think I know everyone you three know."

He turned his attention to Ynna. "A list like that could be very valuable to certain people."

"Lucky for us, we are certain people," Ynna said flatly. She had no interest in selling the list to Killian—a quick buck now would pale in comparison to what they could make from running the jobs themselves.

Killian seemed impressed with the young woman. "I will give you what you need, but you better believe I still get my cut, and I'd better not hear that you tried to fence any goods with anyone else, or this partnership will come to an abrupt and violent end."

He said the last words with an icy truth.

"We know," Whitney said with a cutesy eye roll, but there was fear in her voice.

"Come into the back, and we can find you some gear," Killian offered, gesturing to a door behind the counter. He pointed to Whitney and Ynna. "The stuff I have may not fit right, so you may need to try on a few things for me."

Whitney and Ynna grimaced in unison. "Fuck off, Kil," Whitney snarled.

Killian licked his lips. "Not what you've said before."

Ynna's stomach turned.

"You can watch me change," Metric said, mercifully pulling attention by taking off his shirt. "I've been wanting to show these abs off forever."

"Hard pass," Killian said, standing and punching a code into a keypad by the side of the door.

"I guess I'll just go fuck myself," Pes added angrily.

Killian looked over his shoulder at her, "Oh, I'd still fu—"

"That's my sister!" Metric interrupted.

Killian winked at Pes. "I still would."

As they stepped into the back room, Ynna vowed to one day put Killian in his place.

The room was as big as the shop itself, and Ynna was not surprised that Killian kept it behind a heavy door. The walls, shelves, tables, and boxes were filled and lined with stolen goods. Weapons, ammunition, blueprints, computer parts, and cybernetic augments were everywhere.

For the first time, Ynna realized just how much business Killian actually did. She was so put off by the way he spoke to her that she had been blinded to his business acumen. The moment taught her a lesson she would carry with her the rest of her life—never underestimate a scumbag.

Looking around, Ynna realized what she had been saving for. While she had enjoyed carving out a style for herself, she hadn't been sure what she was waiting to spend her money on.

This was it.

She wanted the tech, the weapons—all of it.

Killian started grabbing light, black armor with masks, and interference equipment to distort camera imaging. He tossed them each some items and made his way over to a wall of guns.

"What you like?" he asked. Then amended, "It'll come out of your earnings."

Metric picked a large, long shotgun, Pes grabbed a handgun, and Whitney a beam gun. Ynna stared at the wall, unsure what to do. She had never handled a weapon in her life, and she had learned in her self-defense class that they were usually far more deadly to the carrier.

She wanted to look tough and took a breath before pulling a black weapon off the wall, startled by the weight of it in her hand.

"SMG, eh?" Killian asked. "Know how to use that thing?"

"No, can you teach me?" she said absently, bouncing it against her palm.

"Oh, I can teach you," he said, and his tone snapped her back.

"She's underage, man," Metric put in, flexing for show and pretending that he wasn't. Whitney was watching and looking at him the way Killian looked at her.

Killian gave a sinister smile. "Age is just a number."

Ynna couldn't hold herself back. "Said every fucking creep ever."

He laughed, caught off guard by her comment.

Ynna smiled with false sweetness. "So, can you teach me?"

"Yes," he said simply.

"I want to be there when you do," Whitney said in such a protective manner she reminded Ynna of her mother.

"I'll be fine," Ynna said gratefully.

"Come by at closing, and I'll take you to learn," Killian offered.

Ynna nodded, and they all took their supplies back to The Press. They had a lockbox there where they could store the stuff. There was an unspoken agreement among the people who stayed there that they would not steal from one another.

Ynna had watched the street justice that followed when one old man broke the rule. The sounds of his bones shattering rang in her ears for days after.

They were all too excited to run any jobs that day, so they spent their time messing around and walking the city streets with Ynna pointing out places they could hit. After scoping out one particularly unguarded shop with a potential weapon cache under the floorboards, they decided to make a go at it the following night.

As the sun was setting and they were parting ways, Whitney offered again, "You sure you don't want me to join you?"

"No," Ynna said, still grateful for the offer. "Killian acts tough, but he's strung-out, and I could break his fingers before he made a grab at me."

Whitney nodded. "He's actually not so bad one on one. He's still disgusting, but he tends to be all talk."

"That's the sense I got," Ynna told her. "Still, I'll keep my eyes open and watch my back."

"Your ass, more like," Whitney half-joked.

"I thought that was implied," Ynna said and shifted her weight, so they bumped shoulders.

WHITNEY WAS RIGHT ABOUT KILLIAN. During the time he walked Ynna to a twenty-four-hour gun range, and while teaching her the proper use of the weapon, he was mostly respectful. Mostly.

He made his typical lewd comments and "accidentally" brushed against her chest or bottom but tended to keep his hands to himself.

Firing a gun for the first time was a jarring experience. The weight was one thing, but when the recoil slammed against Ynna's arm, she realized that she was completely unprepared. Killian laughed as she shook out her arm and showed her how to load clips and stand to brace for the impact.

She was pleased that she had asked for help and that Killian was actually a good teacher.

As they wound down the lesson, he reminded her, "You don't want to have to use this. It's all about the threat and the intimidation. Taking a life—even in self-defense, and even of someone you may think deserves it—stays with you."

She understood that he was right. The violence she had seen with Hector was enough to scar her, and the idea of killing someone unnerved her greatly.

"Thank you for tonight," she said, and she meant it.

He grinned. "You know how you could thank me?"

"Ugh," she groaned. "Just when I thought we were having a nice moment."

"Can't help it," he said, all false innocence.

"Right, the scorpion and the frog," she said, remembering a fable Hector had taught her.

Killian looked perplexed. She clipped the weapon into a sling that he had provided and zipped up her jacket as they exited into the night.

"It's an old story," she told him. "A scorpion wants passage across a river and asks a frog for help. The frog is reluctant, but the scorpion assures him that he won't do anything foolish.

"Halfway across the river, the scorpion stings the frog, ensuring certain death for them both. The frog says, 'Why did you do that? We will both die now.'

"The scorpion answers that he had to do it because it's his nature," she told him.

"Oh," he said, and she detected a slight sadness in his voice. It was the first genuine moment she had ever experienced with him.

"It's just a story," she tried to amend.

"Sure," he said, avoiding eye contact by looking down the street.

"Seriously," she said, putting a hand on his forearm and giving a little squeeze. "Thank you."

He looked into her eyes with a slight smile. "No problem. Don't get yourself killed," he said and turned to walk away.

She smirked, having him right where she wanted him.

CHAPTER 9

Having spent the day doing recon on their target, they felt good about their plan.

Meals In Heels was a food distribution service which received cases of Bio-Meals in the morning and sent scantily clad delivery people out to homes of veterans and the elderly during the day. It was further proof of the rampant sexism which Karen had warned her daughter about. It did not surprise Ynna to learn that the Carcer intel suggested the company also delivered drugs through the business.

LOTP, the pharmaceutical giant, had no competition in the city and sold its medicines for costs that kept people in need from being able to afford anything else. Metric explained that the people who owned the shop either stole or fabricated knock-offs and sold them for slightly cheaper (though still exorbitant) prices.

"Won't the people who need these drugs be fucked if we steal them?" Ynna had asked, wondering if they should pick a different target.

Metric laughed. "If you think they won't replenish the next day, I've got a bridge to sell you."

Whitney chimed in, "This is just one small front for a much larger operation. Whatever we jack is small for them, though it will be a boon for us. Plus, they're gross."

That made Ynna feel better. She did worry about angering whoever owned the shop, but that was going to be inevitable no matter who they robbed.

"So, we all feel good about the plan?" Metric asked.

Heads nodded all around.

"Good," he said.

"Let's start to get rich," Whitney said in a strange robotic voice. She had pulled her black mask over her face, and the audio augmenter worked well.

It was closer to morning than to sunset, and the streets were mostly empty except for the few people smoking and drinking outside of The Sodiac Bar.

They took no note of the four people skulking through the alleys clad in all black, and Ynna was relieved when she saw their target. It looked like every other closed shop on the street: barred windows with the faint glow of electronics flickering within.

Garbage blew down the street in the wind as they made sure the coast was clear.

It was. They ducked behind parked cars and trash cans as they darted toward the storefront. A streetlight flickered, and Ynna's heart nearly burst from her chest.

They all pulled out their weapons as Whitney took the lead with Pes by her side. They looked at one another nervously, though all they could see of each other were the eyes.

Ynna set the lenses to thermal imaging and saw the red visage of the one guard through the wall. She held up one finger to Whitney and nodded. Pes moved up to the door and was now fully illuminated under the streetlight. Whitney stood at her shoulder with her weapon primed. They had watched the guards at the keypad all day and had the code memorized.

If the guard within was watching monitors, all he would see was some slight distortion. Ynna was pleased that Killian had provided such expensive equipment. They all shifted nervously as Pes nodded, too, and punched in the code.

A light flashed red.

"Shit," Pes hissed.

She tried again.

Red.

Metric and Ynna hurried over.

"It isn't working," Pes whispered, fear and disappointment in her words.

Metric stayed calm. "Probably a separate code overnight. Guess we aren't the first to try this."

It made sense, but Ynna was terrified. They were exposed, and this was already taking too long.

Metric produced a tablet and got to work hacking the lock.

Ynna felt the perspiration soak her as she looked up and down the street for any activity.

She turned to watch the screen as it attempted iteration after iteration of the code.

Her heart leaped from her chest as she heard a crunch from down the street, and all eyes turned as a man rounded a corner. Whitney pointed her weapon with a tremulous hand, ready to stun the man. Even as he looked down the street, he didn't seem to notice them.

Metric breathed a sigh of relief as the man swung an arm and Ynna turned to him quizzically.

"AR," Metric told them. "Guy's probably in a castle fighting goblins or something."

Ynna had never been happier with people's addiction to

technology. The man continued past them, his eyes black and augmented ears glowing.

They were as good as invisible.

The relief was short-lived as the lock flashed green.

"Here we go," Pes whispered and pushed the door open.

Whitney burst through with her gun raised.

The man's eyes went wide as the room filled with the white light of Whitney's shot. The beam struck him in the neck, and he began to convulse wildly as the room filled with the smell of burned flesh. His body shook as he fell to the floor, the chair he had been sitting on sliding across the floor.

Whitney was frozen as the others moved in.

Metric walked toward the back door as Ynna looked up from the guard breathing quietly on the ground.

"Metric," she called out, but it was too late.

As he opened the door, a red blur in the lenses leaped toward his neck.

He raised his arms defensively, and the dog bit down on his right forearm. He shrieked with pain, and both Ynna and Pes turned quickly to the door to see if anyone was coming. Whitney snapped out of her trance and fired again, striking Metric in the back. His armor dissipated the shot, but enough was left to make him go rigid.

The dog thrashed, sending spit and blood spraying around the room. Pes rushed over to try and pull the creature off, but it was no use.

"Out of the way," Whitney cried and fired just as Pes stepped aside.

The beam hit the dog, and the massive amount of energy loosed his grip instantly. Metric and the dog collapsed to the floor together, the animal breathing shallowly.

Blood seeped down Metrics arm. He was pale, and his eyes wild.

"We have to get out of here," Pes screamed.

"Get him moving toward The Press, we'll get the goods and be right behind," Ynna said. Whitney looked rattled but nodded vigorously.

Pes looked at her in shock. "You want to stay?"

"This isn't going to be for nothing, now get him moving," Ynna ordered, and Pes helped her brother to his feet.

Ynna turned to Whitney. "Come on, Friendly Fire," she said and gave her a little slap.

Whitney blinked and followed Ynna to the back room.

Wire rack shelving units filled the space, and Ynna switched her lenses to a mode that Rose had programmed and called "blueprint variation detection."

Rose had explained that she had created it to find hidden spots around the school to hide but that it could be used to spot hidden compartments in buildings. That had been the moment Ynna had truly accepted that Rose was wise to her plan.

The lenses displayed a digital image of what the building should be, overlaid with what it was. A place under a floorboard glowed an incandescent white. Ynna knelt and saw a bent nail worn smooth and pulled it, the wood board coming up on a hinge.

"Whoa," Whitney murmured.

Ynna looked up at her from the plastic bags filled with pills. "Your standing around looking pretty days are over, hand me that fucking duffle," she barked.

Whitney sulked. "You're mean under pressure."

"I'd rather be mean than slow," Ynna said, raising a hand expectantly.

Whitney unslung the bag from her back and handed it down.

"I'll watch your back," Whitney said, turning to face the door.

"Don't you mean my ass?" Ynna joked.

Whitney looked over her shoulder, her eyes smiling under the mask. "I thought that was implied."

Ynna chuckled as she put the last of the bags into the duffle.

"Let's get the fuck out of here," she said, standing and moving toward the door.

"You'll get no argument from me," Whitney agreed as they moved through the store onto the street.

"Hey!" A voice boomed at them from an idling truck.

"Shit!" Whitney exclaimed as she started running, Ynna right behind.

They heard the truck accelerate quickly in their direction.

They ducked into a narrow alleyway, hopping over trash bags and empty crates as they made their escape. Ynna had never been so scared or exhilarated in her life.

When they reached The Press, it was quiet. The smell of baking bread from one electric oven filled their noses. Thick wires coiled like vines up to the roof to a solar panel that powered the oven.

Once inside the security of the building, Whitney pulled her mask off and turned with a smile to Ynna.

She embraced her. "We did it," Whitney whispered in her ear, and a man sleeping under a plastic tarp shifted at the noise.

"Let's check on Met," Ynna said, pulling away.

She was pleased that they had been successful but loathed the mistakes.

She pulled away from the hug and moved to their corner, where Pes was wrapping Metric's arm.

He looked up at them. "Actually, it isn't so bad. The armor did its thing." He gave them a weak smile.

Whitney rushed over to hug him, knocking him back into the couch.

"I'm so sorry," she pleaded for forgiveness.

"It's okay," he soothed. "We did great for our first time."

"There is a lot we can learn from this," Ynna pointed out, and the others ignored her. They seemed too happy at the prospect of their earnings to care what she had to say. "Good job, everyone," she amended. There would be time later to discuss their mistakes.

"Sure," Pes snorted, but Whitney and Metric smiled.

Once they had wrapped Metric's wound and stashed their loot, Pes produced an unmarked jug of brown liquid. The jug moved around the circle a few times, and before long, they were all joking and laughing, red-faced and red-eyed.

YNNA SNEEZED HERSELF AWAKE, and her head throbbed worse than it ever had in her life.

She turned to vomit and saw a drying stain next to where she lay. She knew it had been a long night and morning.

"Shit," she mumbled to herself, wiping her lips.

The smell of sick filled her nose. She looked around and saw her armored clothes neatly folded nearby. Looking down, she realized she was in a long shirt, soaked in sweat with a unicorn on the front.

"You said it'd look good with your hair," Pes chuckled, and Ynna blinked to bring her into focus.

Her hand was extended with a cup of steaming liquid.

Ynna took it graciously. "Thanks."

"No problem," Pes said. "Both our parents were drunks, so we can hold our liquor. Same can't be said for you two."

She nodded over Ynna's shoulder, and she turned to see Whitney and Metric in a sleeping bag with clothes strewn all about them.

"She finally told him how she felt last night," Pes informed her. "It's been obvious for so long, but boys are stupid and need to be hit over the head with that shit."

Ynna nodded. Even the slight movement sent waves of pain through her head. She sipped at the coffee and tasted the booze mixed in.

Pes saw the reaction and smirked. "Hair of the dog."

"Right," Ynna croaked and sent the rest of the cup down her gullet.

She looked back at Whitney and smiled, happy her friend had finally gotten what she wanted, even if she wouldn't remember it.

"Just chip my earnings. I have to check in with my mom," Ynna said to Pes.

"We got you," Pes smiled, and Ynna turned on shaky legs.

"Thanks," Ynna said over her shoulder as she left.

SHE STOPPED at the apartment to splash water on her face, wash the puke from her hair, and change.

When she reached the diner, Karen rushed out from behind the counter and wrapped her up.

"I was so worried," she told Ynna.

She gripped her daughter's shoulders and moved to appraise her. "You look as bad as you smell."

"Sorry, mom," Ynna said with a hangdog expression. "Just out with friends."

To Ynna's surprise, her mom smiled. "I'm just happy you're alright. And I'm happy you are making friends. But if you are going to be out all-night drinking, you have to tell me."

Ynna chuckled. "Fair enough."

Karen stared at her. "You're getting so grown up."

Ynna groaned with embarrassment. "Oh, mom."

"It's true," Karen said. "You think we could have dinner

together this weekend? Maybe you could stop by here, and I could take a long break."

"Sure." Ynna smiled. "That would be nice."

"Good," Karen affirmed. "It's a date. I think I want to get to know this new you."

"I'm still just me, mom," Ynna told her.

Karen reached out and put a hand on Ynna's cheek. "Oh, honey. Your lies may have worked on your father, but they never worked on me."

Ynna laughed. "I know."

"Anyway, it's also..." Karen began.

"Also, what?"

"It's also your birthday," Karen told her.

Ynna thought about it.

She was right.

Ynna had been so consumed with Hector and her plans that she had entirely neglected her own birthday. She laughed to herself that a cheap dinner and a piece of pie with her mother sounded like a perfect celebration.

For her sixteenth, her father had rented the most expensive ballroom at the Van Orlock Hotel, hiring steam machines and holoprojectors to turn the dance floor into an Amazon jungle. Robot jaguars stalked the floors, and guests fed cloned sloths. The adults drank and took drugs, pretending to chaperone while the teens pretended not to drink and do drugs.

It had been the peak of opulence, and now, standing in a decrepit diner with stained floors, Ynna couldn't imagine a worse party.

CHAPTER 10

The next week was the most thrilling and terrifying of Ynna's life. She spent her days scouting targets and her nights robbing them. Even after dividing the profits four ways and giving Killian his cut, they all took home more money than they had in the past several months.

They were getting more confident with each job and taking the time to plan for the unexpected. They had a swagger when walking into The Press, and they were happy.

Things had progressed with Metric and Whitney, too. After their night together, Ynna had caught them making eyes at each other, holding hands, and stealing kisses when they thought no one was looking.

Ynna thought it was cute and pulled Whitney aside after a job one night to say, "I'm really happy for you."

Whitney beamed. "It's kinda your fault."

Ynna blanched. "How's that?"

"When you first showed up, you know I was jealous. I didn't like that you are prettier, and when you came up with this genius plan, I didn't like that you were smarter, too.

"But I saw that you were determined to get what you wanted

and in some drunken haze, decided to be like you. Without meaning to, you inspired me."

Ynna felt her face flush. "I'm happy it worked out."

"It really did. And," Whitney checked to make sure Metric was out of earshot, "you've inspired us all. We talk about it all the time. Met will always think of himself as our leader, and it's best if he does, but we were floundering before you came along. Now, we have a purpose, cash in our pockets, and a true leader."

Ynna could hardly take the compliments.

She knew Whitney was correct and had felt herself becoming a strong woman, but hearing it put to words was almost too much.

"Thank you for saying that," Ynna said, and she meant it.

"Killian also says you're becoming a really good shot," Whitney added.

Ynna agreed. "I've been going with him every day, and I'm getting better. It's funny, my whole life I've been just okay at things. I mean, I was popular but never particularly good at school or sports or anything. But now, for the first time, I feel like I've found something I do well."

Whitney smiled and gave her a pat on the backside. "You have, and you lift the rest of us to your level."

Ynna let her face fall flat. "Thanks for that."

Whitney smirked. "Any time."

"I'm going to take tomorrow night off," Ynna said, changing the subject. "Going to have dinner with my mom."

"Ooh, la la," Whitney joked and made a knowing face. "Celebrating the big birthday?"

"What?" Ynna shrieked. "How do you know that?"

"I didn't say you were the *only* clever one in this little crew," Whitney was trying to hold back her brimming elation.

"Fine," Ynna said. "So you know the secret. Just don't get me anything, okay?"

"Too late!" Whitney squealed.

She handed Ynna an envelope.

"It's from all of us," Whitney told her.

Ynna looked at Whitney, her heart full. "Thank you. For everything."

"Sappy isn't a good look on you. Just open it," Whitney said, but it was obvious that she was happy.

Ynna opened the card. Handwritten inside was a brief note saying, "To the baddest bitch on the block. Now you can conquer the world in style." Beneath the words was a printed barcode and logo of a hair salon.

"We all know you want a microdye, so we pooled our money to get you this. Nanite technology at its finest: being used for woman's fashion," Whitney joked, but they both knew that it was as thoughtful a gift, as it was expensive.

Ynna just stared at it, her eyes welling. "It's too much."

Whitney let out a laugh. "Shit, man. You're the only reason we were able to afford it!"

"Thanks," was all she could muster, and she pulled her mask on to cover the tears.

THE RUN WENT SMOOTHLY, but Ynna could not sleep well on the eve of her birthday. She was consumed with conflicting emotions. She hadn't slept well since Hector had been taken, and the combination of fear and joy made her restless.

She rolled over, thinking she heard a noise.

In a half-asleep daze, she looked around the room and noticed the door was open.

Her heart raced as she tried to remember if she had left it open for the cat. Everything was still in its place as she stood cautiously, Karen snoring under the covers.

Her mother slept well, perpetually exhausted from working as much as she did.

Ynna made her way out the door to see the window open. Gato was nowhere in sight. She let out a sigh. He had no doubt awakened her as he got up to leave on a morning hunt. There was no shortage of mice for him to bring back and present to her as a bloody gift.

Knowing the fitful couple of hours was all she would get, she admitted defeat and fired up her gaming console.

After a while, as the sun began to streak through the room, Karen entered.

"You were up early," she observed groggily.

Ynna put down the controller. "Yeah, there's coffee on."

Karen nodded and plodded over to the kitchen. "We still on for tonight?"

Ynna smiled. "Wouldn't miss it. Gonna get my hair done, and I'll be over."

"That's a nice treat for yourself," Karen said through a yawn.

"I thought so," Ynna agreed, still not sure about sharing her new friends with her mother.

"Happy birthday, honey," Karen said and made her way over to kiss her daughter on the head.

Ynna smiled.

THE MACHINE that dyed her hair hurt, and she hated the entire process. The spider-like robotic spikes poking and prodding her hair forced her to shift uncomfortably, and she winced as the style technician covered his mouth to keep from laughing.

As the arms lifted away from her head, retracting and folding like an umbrella, Ynna caught sight of herself in the mirror. Aside from a few streaks of blood from her scalp, she loved the new look. She shook her head slightly, and a sparkling shimmer flowed through her bright pink hair.

"Suits you," the technician observed before smirking. "In a streetwalker sort of way."

Ynna snorted. She had spent her whole life around people who thought they were better than everyone and found it incredibly distasteful.

She had seen the way he had looked at her when she walked in—like some creature that dragged itself from the depths for one taste of luxury.

She smiled as she produced the card, causing him to grimace.

"You win this in a giveaway?" he asked in so patronizing a tone that she wanted to wheel around and slap him.

She smirked. "Something like that."

He ran a scanner over the barcode and looked at her expectantly.

"A tip," he said, extending a flat palm.

"Sure, here's your fucking tip—don't be a smug, superior dick to people," she said. It was an old line, but one she was happy to use.

She pulled the lead vest off and jammed it in his hand, snatching back the card and nearly skipping from the shop. She knew she should wait for instructions on how and when to wash and maintain it, but she could look all that up and was happy to be leaving with a win.

The salon was on the Main Street of the district, and she smiled at all the passing shoppers who looked on her with disdain. She remembered sitting with her old friends as they mocked other girls for what they wore. Now, she simply smiled at the same type of snooty bitches as they judged her.

She caught the bus back to her neighborhood and disembarked as the sun was setting. She strode over to D&M Jones's

Diner, where she saw her mother wiping down a table with a dirty rag. When it had been built, the diner had been styled to look old, a throwback to another era. Now it was just old.

The cherry top seats were ripped, the checkered floor was peeling, and the silver metal adornments were coated in brown rust. A fluorescent light flickered in a rounded display—pieces of pie cooked who-knows-when sitting on a wire rack.

The cook nodded from a filthy cooktop as she entered.

"Karen, your kid's here," he bellowed. "Your thirty starts now."

She dropped her rag into a plastic rectangle of what was supposed to be clean water and gestured at a booth.

"Hey, honey," she said to Ynna before turning to the cook. "Bill, two burgers whenever you finish there."

He pulled one hand from his trousers, gave his fingers a sniff, and nodded.

Ynna frowned.

"Just tell yourself the heat will cook off any bacteria," Karen suggested, catching her daughter's look.

"That work?"

Karen smirked. "Not really."

Ynna chuckled. "How you doing, Mom?"

"I'm okay, honey. But more importantly, how are you doing? I love the new look," she said, and Ynna could tell her mom wanted to ask where she got the money.

"Thanks. I do, too," Ynna said, not interested in giving her what she wanted.

"That's good," Karen said with a warm but weak smile. "So, tell me, what's going on? Tell me about yourself. I see you growing and changing, and I hardly recognize you anymore. I want to get to know you again."

Ynna smiled, too. It was sweet that her mom was making such an effort, and Ynna told her about her life. She explained that Hector had introduced her to some work opportunities and that she was making friends. Karen didn't press her on the work but wanted to know all about Pes, Metric, and Whitney.

She seemed thrilled that her daughter was making a life for herself while throwing in some choice words about the value of education.

The food came, and they chatted while Ynna chewed dubiously. They spent much longer than Karen's allotted break, but with no customers in sight, the cook didn't seem bothered.

As she finished the last bite of a banana cream pie, Karen looked at her seriously.

"Honey," she began. "You know I don't have much money, but I thought that this year, instead of buying you a crappy gift, I would give you something you've always wanted."

Ynna was intrigued. "Okay."

"From now on, I'm going to try to call you Ynna," she said, turning her fork in her fingers. "It won't be easy, and it may take some time, but you are a woman now. A strong woman and one who deserves to be called the name she chooses."

"Oh," Ynna said, and for the second time in as many days, she felt tears begin to wet her eyes.

"I've never told you this, and you have to understand that it's hard for me, but I could never call you it because of your brother," Karen's words were getting caught in her throat, and she was trying to hold back tears of her own.

"I figured. It's just—" Ynna began, but Karen held up a trembling hand.

"I know you call yourself Ynna to honor him. I understand that it means something to you, but for all these years, when I heard it, I've only heard his voice. I've heard him struggle to say Marina, and I couldn't bring myself to say it, too. He was so young when—when he died.

"And just like you with all this, I couldn't help but blame

myself. I know logically that I couldn't have stopped him from falling down those stairs. I know that it was an accident. But a mother can't help but feel—can't help but blame herself."

Silence oppressed them as she stopped speaking. Ynna had no words. She just watched her mother weep. She stood and moved to the other side of the table, wrapping her arm around Karen.

"I love you, honey," Karen squeaked. "I want to honor him, too, and I think it's time."

"Okay, mom," Ynna whispered as she rested her head on her mom's shoulder. "I love you, too."

The bell on the diner door rang, and the two women turned. Ynna's heart pounded as she saw a beefy man with one robotic leg and a ski mask over his face holding a charged gun. Ynna reached before realizing she had left her weapon at The Press.

It was for the best, she decided. Robberies were common, and she didn't need to start a gun battle.

"Transfer everything you have on sight to this chip," he demanded of the cook. The man's eyes darted around wildly. "And some pie, I want some fucking pie!" he demanded. Ynna knew that some addicts needed sugar when they were coming down from a high.

The cook caught the chip in one hand and moved slowly to the register. "We don't make much, look at this place."

The man with the gun moved forward threateningly. "Just give me what you got!"

He sounded nervous, and Ynna wondered if it was his first time. For a brief moment, she had sympathy for him, remembering how worried she had been. She clutched her mother tight.

The cook plugged the chip into the computer, typing nervously on the screen. "It will take a while, this piece of shit is old, and Carcer will be here any moment."

"I know you don't have Carcer protection," the man stated.

Ynna's heart nearly stopped, and rage filled her as she realized. Killian had looked into her eyes when he played wounded that night at the firing range. He had played her. He must have seen the lenses.

It wasn't Gato in the night. It was some hired breaker.

She was so angry. She wanted to leap up and beat the armed man to death. She hated Killian. She hated herself for thinking she was smart.

"Here," the cook said, pulling out the chip.

As the man moved forward, the cook pulled a pistol from under the counter.

"No!" Ynna found herself yelling as the two men fired at once. Sound and light like thunder and lightning filled the space in an instant.

Both men were knocked back, and as he fell, the armed man's body twitched—an involuntary death throw that was enough to pull the trigger of his weapon as he reeled back.

Brightness filled the room again, and Ynna blinked several times to regain her vision.

Her mother looked at Ynna, her eyes wide with shock.

Ynna looked down to see Karen's hands move to the smoking hole through her ribs.

"Mom!" she wailed and pressed her hands over her mother's.

She remembered how she felt that morning with her brother, how he had been playing with that toy dropship at the top of the stairs before losing his balance. Ynna had rushed to him as he tipped over the edge, watching his body contort and break as he fell.

The color drained from her mother's face just as it had with her brother.

Ynna screamed as she had then.

A tear streaked down her face as Karen looked at her daughter one last time. "I love you, Ynna."

The words came out heavy, and her head fell under its own weight.

Ynna stopped screaming. The room was silent except for the soft jazz still playing from the jukebox.

Her whole body shook.

The thief was dead.

The cook was dead.

Her mother was dead.

SHE STOOD IN A DAZE, looking down at the corpse that had only a moment before been the only person in this world who loved her.

She knew she should wait. Wait to see her mother taken away. Wait to tell the officers what had happened.

She couldn't.

She heard her own voice say, "I love you too, mom." She pulled the necklace she had rescued from their house from her mother's neck and jammed it in a pocket, knowing she would never sell it.

Her shaky legs carried her out through the blurred gaggle of onlookers and down the neon streets. Familiar faces were as strangers as she entered The Press. Her friends were not there.

Dried blood flaked from her hands as she pulled the machinegun free.

She made no attempt to hide it as she stalked toward the pawnshop.

CHAPTER 11

Two thugs waited in front of the darkened shop as Ynna approached, her weapon raised.

"Whoa, there, girly," one said as the two lifted their hands defensively.

In a rage, she fired a burst and blazed the face of the one who had spoken. Blood cascaded into the air as the other man rushed forward, spearing her in the stomach with his shoulder. She gasped for air and saw white as he wrestled the weapon free and picked her up with ease, clutching both her wrists in one massive hand.

She thrashed, trying to remember her training, but she was too weak and drained to do much of anything. The brute dragged her inside where Killian was waiting for her. He smiled —a wicked, evil grin.

"I knew I would get you to come," Killian said, and the thug at her back chuckled.

"Fuck you! I hate you!" Ynna screamed.

"Bit of an overreaction, my dear," he hissed. He obviously didn't know what stealing Ynna's tech had cost her, but she wasn't thinking of that now. She just wanted to see him hurt or dead.

She flailed again, and the massive man wrapped a hand around her neck and lifted her off her feet.

"I'll. Kill. You," she wheezed.

Killian's grin broadened. "You'll do no such thing. What you *will* do is disappear. You'll crawl back into whatever hole you came from and never bother me again. You'll cut all ties with my employees and go away, or—" and he clicked his tongue against the roof of his mouth. "Or they will find pieces of you all around the city."

She tried to speak, tried to tell him what she would do to him, but she could only gasp weakly for air as the corners of her vision blurred.

Killian stood and moved closer. She tried to kick at him, but her legs were weak and flaccid.

"You young assholes think you're all so smart. You think you can run these streets and cut old Killian out, but I'll tell you something—I've run these streets since before you were a set of options on some doctor's screen. I've survived raids and riots. I've pulled through more than you can ever know and come out on top.

"I thought getting rid of Hector would show you your place, but instead, it somehow made you better."

He shook his head disapprovingly. She tried to thrash again at Hector's name, but she had nothing left. Even as he spoke, Killian was a fog. "Now, you have given me more than I ever thought possible, and your use to me has come to an end... so unless you want to give me the other thing I want, you can go away."

Ynna felt herself fall to the floor. She sputtered and gasped.

"I'll never give you anything," she forced.

Killian frowned. "Then it was a pleasure doing business with you."

She didn't even feel the baton strike her head.

YNNA AWOKE in a state of misery she had never imagined possible.

The new life she had made for herself was gone, shattered in less than an hour. Her body shook, and she sobbed uncontrollably for what felt like an hour. Her face hurt from being pulled into a mask of misery.

Eventually, she stopped crying long enough to breathe— small rasping breaths that caught in her chest. She looked around to get her bearings, dark clouds dumping thudding rain onto her. She was covered in mud and saw an overpass above her. Her battered body tried to force itself from the ground, but she slipped and fell back into the mud that already coated her.

She felt the fresh wounds and bruises she had no doubt acquired from being dumped in this drainage ditch.

Blood soaked into the dirt as she scrambled up the hill and onto the street above. A lamp overhead flickered in the rain.

She looked up the street, seeing bars with prostitutes standing under awnings. At the end of the road, a taxi waited with a green light at the top. She felt for her cash chip and, finding it, moved as quickly as she could to the vehicle.

She threw herself in and let out a sigh before coughing blood into her filthy hand.

Later, she would wonder how different her life might have turned out if she had decided to go to Rose at that moment, but delirious and exhausted, Ynna entered the only address she knew by heart.

THE HOUSE she had known her whole life looked unfamiliar and ominous as the cab set down. She moved as quickly as her body would take her to the front door and punched in the combination.

She couldn't help but chuckle that her father had closed their accounts before they were even out the door but hadn't taken the time to change the locks.

As the door opened, a beautiful, perfect-looking woman who Ynna assumed was another relief aid, stood before her in the foyer.

"Marina Hawkins, you are authorized as a guest of the household, you may follow me," the woman said with a flat affect. She turned, and Ynna followed the thing, hints of bare ass peeking out from under the skirt with each step.

The massive dining room was all but empty as she entered. Her father sat with half-finished steak, a glass of scotch, and cigar. He was the physical embodiment of privilege.

He looked up at her briefly and winced, his eyes instantly shifting away from his child. "You look appalling."

Ynna felt her eyes burn. She was wounded, broken both inside and out, and all he cared about was how she looked. She realized then that she not only hated him but that he was a truly bad person. She had known it but had held out some sliver of hope for him.

"Mom's dead," she tried, thinking that maybe, just maybe, she could elicit some kind of reaction.

He raised his glass in mock cheers. "I know. Carcer came just before you with images for me to identify. I made arrangements for her."

She saw the steak, drink, and cigar in a new light—he was celebrating.

To go from Killian to this was almost too much. She wanted to see positivity or hope in the world and was only met with the worst that humanity had to offer. As she tried to formulate words, to figure out what to say to the man, another woman entered. To her disgust, she saw that the machine was modeled after one of her schoolmates who her father had always taken a particular interest in. The replica wasn't perfect, no doubt scammed from images in Ynna's room, but the resemblance was clear. She wore nothing but an apron and strode over to clear the plate from the table.

Melvin didn't acknowledge her except to lean back to let her take the dish. He spoke without looking up. "What is it that you want?"

Ynna had been asking herself the same question. She had come to this place thinking it would feel safe, but being here had only made her feel worse. "I need help, dad."

She hung her head in shame.

He snorted. "So, money?"

She shook her head. That's all that mattered to him. Watching the robot sway from the room, she had no words.

"I'll book you a room at BA General," he offered as though he was the most altruistic man on the planet and bringing up a screen on the table. "After that, I think it would be best if we part ways."

On that, they agreed. "Fine."

She turned to leave, happy to be rid of this place and this man. "And Ynna," he said. He had never had any qualms calling her by that name. She turned back, unable to help but let the hope return. "I mean it, don't come back here."

"That won't be a problem." Ynna snorted, vowing never to see the man again.

WITH JUST THE passage of a short time, her body was so achy that she could barely walk to the cab that she had been wise enough to have wait for her. After lurching in, she opened the window to vomit out the side, the bile burning her throat. She input the Biological Damage wing of BA General and was off, the cab lifting into the dark night.

Her father had paid the least amount he could for her recovery, and she huddled in a corner of the brightly lit, overcrowded waiting room before a drudge called her name. She drifted in and out of consciousness as the prescribed drugs and exhaustion took a toll on her battered body.

She had no visitors, and the loneliness was more brutal than the recovery. Doctors filtered through, each one making snide remarks about how she should change her lifestyle.

After providing a fingerprint to close out her bill, she left the hospital a few days later with a plan. She knew it was risky, but also knew she had to do something. She would need money to start a new life, but she also knew she could no longer run jobs in Redwood Point.

SHE APPROACHED The Press from the outside, careful to go unseen. It was quiet at night as all of the activity was happening within. She moved some crates to form a little staircase and lifted the cracked window by her gang's spot. She saw Pes watching a movie on the old screen, and she cleared her throat. Pes looked up, and sadness crossed her face.

"No," Pes said, looking forlorn.

"Please," Ynna whispered.

Pes shook her head. "Ynna, I'm sorry, we can't risk it."

At the sound of Pes's voice, Whitney came around a corner with Metric, sweaty and disheveled.

"Ynna?" Whitney burst out and ran over to the window, beckoning her inside.

"Killian will kill us," Pes warned.

Whitney looked at her with disgust. "Killian can suck my dick."

"Your funeral." Pes threw her hands up and turned back to the screen.

Metric looked worried but didn't say anything as Whitney reached up to help Ynna through the window. She landed easily, feeling no pain.

Whitney wrapped her up in a hug. "We heard what happened at the diner. I'm so sorry."

"Thanks," Ynna said, trying to push the image out of her mind.

"Killian warned us not to contact you," she told Ynna.

"I figured." Ynna nodded. "Told me the same thing about you."

"We figured," Whitney said.

Metric came over and gave Ynna a little hug, too, all the time watching to make sure no one was watching them.

"How you holding up?" Metric asked genuinely, but it was plain to Ynna that he was not excited by her return.

"Been better, but I think I have a job that can change our lives forever," Ynna said with a smile.

"Wow, same old Ynna," Whitney chided playfully.

"I'm guessing your fortunes have changed?" Ynna asked.

Whitney nodded. "Since Kil stole your info, he charges for information on places to hit. We remembered a couple, but after it was too risky. Good jobs cost too much for us, and after the first night, the local merchants seemed to get wise. Carcer salesmen are patrolling the streets, and everyone wants the protection now."

Ynna snorted. "Guess they got what they wanted."

"What's that?" Metric asked.

"The database was super easy to hack. Carcer wanted someone to find the list so they could increase their business."

"That's fucked up, so it makes perfect sense," Whitney shook her head. "So, what's this job?"

"ARE WE CLOSE ENOUGH?" Ynna asked Pes the following night as they pressed their black-clad bodies against a tall, decorative wall. She had spent the previous day wandering the streets and snagging sleep where she could. With her mother dead, the apartment had been turned back to the ownership company, so Ynna had no place in the world where she could rest. She was tired and worn out, but knew that when they were successful, she could rent herself a room somewhere.

"Yes," Pes said, pulling out her tablet in the dark. The screen glowed blue in the fog that breathed heavily down the street. It had taken a lot of cajoling for Whitney to convince Pes to come along, but now that she was here, she was focused on the job at hand.

Ynna watched as one by one, Pes remotely shut down the relief aids.

"You said one looks like an old friend?" Whitney asked.

"So gross, right?" Ynna snorted.

Metric chuckled. "I think a lot of people use them that way."

"And thank you for the male opinion no one wanted," Whitney mocked.

Even as they joked, Ynna could hear the worry in their voices. It had taken a lot of convincing to get them to come, but the promise of vast wealth had been enough to convince them. The French maid had been wearing one of her mother's bracelets, and Ynna had realized her father had not sold off their belongings.

It made sense to her. Her father had so much money that it would have been more work to sell than he cared to put in.

While he spent long hours at the office, she knew her father to be a lazy man, unwilling to do more than he had to.

"All off," Pes said before adding, "there are a lot of them."

"Of course there are," Ynna seethed.

Pes looked concerned. "And you're sure you can shut off the security?"

Ynna nodded. "Fucker didn't bother to change the codes."

"And you're sure he won't notice the things are gone?" Metric asked.

Ynna had been over this several times already but still wanted to assuage her friend's fears. "Trust me. He doesn't care about these things."

They all nodded dubiously.

Metric helped them over the wall, and Ynna rushed up to the house, pressed the code, and moved quickly to the security panel. She shut off the house's security and used her lenses to scan for life. Though there were many statuesque human forms, there were no people.

Her father never missed his poker nights, and tonight was clearly no exception.

"Come on," she said, and the others winced. She rolled her eyes. "This place is a palace, and there is no one nearby to hear us."

They seemed unconvinced. "Fine," Ynna whispered. "Upstairs."

She guided them to her parents' room, and they all stopped, mouths agape. A naked woman was tied to the bedposts, unblinking and frozen in time.

"Rich people are so fucking weird," Pes observed.

Metric stared until Whitney slapped him on the chest. "You can't have her."

"Oh, no, I—" he stammered before she let out a laugh.

"I'm just fucking with you." She smirked. "Gawk at the disgusting robot all you want."

"Oh," he said, sounding relieved.

"Just know you won't get the real thing for a while," she said, and his head dropped.

"Can we hurry this thing along?" Pes asked.

"Agreed," Ynna said. "You'll have time for all your lover's spats at our new penthouse."

They all seemed to like the sound of that.

Ynna guided them into her mother's closet. It looked almost exactly like how she had left it when she ransacked it for valuables.

As she made her way to the safe nestled behind a coatrack, she turned back to see Whitney running her hands along the dresses. She caught Ynna watching.

"Can I?" she asked.

"Just not too many," Ynna smiled as Whitney pulled the lavish dresses down and jammed them into her bag.

Ynna tried a combination on the safe.

"I thought you said it might take a while, that you didn't know the code," he observed.

"I didn't, it was just a lucky guess," she said, holding back tears. She couldn't bring herself to tell them that the code was her brother's birthday.

They all stood in awe as the heavy door swung open.

The safe was full of diamonds, pearls, gold, and silver. Bracelets, necklaces, earrings, and rings filled the small space, displayed as if in a jewelry shop window.

"Holy shit," Pes said, unable to restrain herself.

Ynna smiled. She had taken some good stuff when she left, but these were the real valuables.

They all grabbed handfuls like kids in a candy shop, jamming their pockets with wealth beyond belief. They smiled and laughed as they tried things on and held them up to themselves. For the first time since Ynna had met them, they were all acting their age.

"And we can all just share these?" Metric asked as if he could not believe his luck.

"Yep," Ynna affirmed, happy to share her wealth with her new friends.

"This is going to change our lives," Whitney gasped. She turned to look at Ynna. "Thank you."

Ynna smiled.

As they neared the front door, pockets and bags full, they were all in as good a mood as they had ever been. Metric had his arm over Whitney, and even Pes was smiling broadly.

That changed in an instant as they opened the door.

Stepping out of the house, they were met with lights and screaming.

"On the ground, now!" a voice barked, and it was all over.

"Fucking bitch," Pes hissed at Ynna as the officers swarmed around them, pointing guns and shackling their hands.

"We have bounties out on all of you," a man announced, pointing a screen at them with pictures of their faces next to monetary values for their arrests.

Ynna's eyes went wide as she read the screen. The moment she saw the officers, she had assumed that her father had put advanced security on the house, but now she saw the truth. Killian had paid for their arrest.

She realized that he must have had them tracked and felt betrayed when they had met with Ynna. Her heart broke once more as she realized that by going to see them, she had doomed her friends.

When he found out what had happened, she assumed her

father would add another bounty to ensure that none of them saw freedom for a very long time.

She hated Killian. Hated Carcer. Hated her father.

All she had ever wanted was to do something good and kind, and all that she had seen was evil.

As they were loaded into a prisoner transport, Ynna looked to Whitney.

"I'm sorry," she pleaded.

But her friend looked at her with a coldness she had never seen before. "Fuck you."

CHAPTER 12

No one spoke to Ynna as the transport flew for what felt like hours.

As the vehicle banked, they all looked out of the barred window and saw it: a city surrounded by walls and towers. It was ugly and imposing.

"No," Ynna whispered to herself.

They weren't being taken to the local prison, but to Carcer City, the massive prison city where people were brought to live out their days as inmates.

She turned, wanting to apologize once more, but the look of pure hatred on the three faces around her kept her quiet.

They didn't speak to her as they were offloaded and processed, given striped uniforms with prisoner numbers written on them.

As she was forced through the door of the administrative building and onto a street surrounded by ramshackle buildings and threatening looking people, she realized that she was truly alone in the world. She didn't know where to go, and couldn't find the people she had counted as friends just moments before.

She slumped against a wall, crumpled to the ground, and put her head on her knees.

SHE DID NOT KNOW how much time had passed when she heard a familiar voice. "Ynna?"

Looking up, she nearly burst.

She leaped to her feet and jumped into Hector's waiting arms.

"What? How did you find me?" she asked. The prison city had looked humongous from the air, and the fact that he was standing before her seemed beyond improbable.

He smiled his old, warm smile. "I watch the bounty boards very close. Many do. I watch for your name, and I watch Killian. Not hard to find you."

"Oh, Hector," she said and squeezed him tight, her tears pouring into his shoulder.

"Where is Karen?" he asked, and the tears began anew.

He nodded gravely and said, "Let us go to speak."

He guided her in silence through the streets. Though she paid little attention to the world around her, she noted that it didn't look that different from Redwood Point. The buildings were short and shoddy and had citizens milling about in front of them. The only difference was that everyone was dressed the same. In the city, personal fashion was important to almost everyone, and here, the uniform sameness was oppressive.

He walked her to the Alco-Traz, a prison-themed saloon. Metal cups and plates were used exclusively, and pictures of prisons lined the walls.

"Poor taste, eh?" Hector joked morosely. He was smiling kindly at her, but she could tell that he was overcome with sadness at the death of her mother. His eyes looked like pools of misery.

Ynna simply nodded as he sat her in a seat. Hector held up two fingers, and cold beers were set before them in an instant.

"What has happened?" Hector asked quietly.

Ynna was silent a long time, using her thumbnail to peel the label off of her beer. "Mom was killed, and it was all my fault. My friends were arrested, and it's all my fault. Everything I touch turns to shit."

Hector put his arm over Ynna's shoulder.

"The world doesn't work like that. These things, they are not your fault," Hector told her. "Things happen. We cannot control them."

"Doesn't feel that way," she said, still unable to look up. "It feels like every decision I make fucks up the world for good people. Then people like my fucking father," she spit on the floor. "Assholes like him take advantage and never suffer."

She was quiet a long moment, thinking about her mother in those last moments. The memory was already fragmented, as though her mind didn't want her to be able to recall it. Hector cleared his throat, and she looked at him, her eyes welling once more.

"I never tell you this," he began. "But you know what your mother say about you?"

"What?" Ynna said, looking into his big eyes.

"She says she think you are destined for greatness. She worked so hard so you can do something in this world. And, knowing you as I do, I agree with her."

Ynna couldn't help but laugh. Everything had gone wrong, and every decision she had made had hurt the people she cared about. "I'm a fuckup."

Hector smiled at her. "No. As I tell you before, you just need a purpose."

Ynna rolled her eyes. "Some good sage wisdom is going to do me in here."

"You are in here now, yes, but not forever. You will get out and do good. I know it, and Karen knew it," he told her. There was no doubt in his voice. He said it as though it were the truest thing he had ever said.

Ynna shook her head in disbelief.

"Trust me, Ynna," he told her, squeezing her shoulder. "I have met many people in this life, but none like you."

She wanted to laugh in his face, call him crazy, but his sincerity quieted the instinct.

"Hector?" she said.

"Yes, dear?"

"What did my mom do for you?" she asked. She couldn't talk about some absurd destiny anymore. She just wanted to know what had bonded him and her mother.

"Ah, is boring story, really. After she get out of the Point, I got in trouble. Big trouble. I never know how she found out, but she hire lawyer and protect me."

"That's it?" Ynna exclaimed. "All the secrecy and everything just for that?"

He shrugged with a wry smile. "Sorry to disappoint."

"I mean, I assumed you were at least lovers or something," Ynna said, drinking the piss-tasting beer for the first time.

"What your mother and I share is more complicated than all that," Hector explained with a faraway look.

She scoffed. "Okay."

"Perhaps you understand when older," he said.

After a while, he asked for more details, and Ynna explained the whole story and how she had ended up in Carcer City. He listened quietly, occasionally asking for more information or swearing in Spanish at the mention of Killian's name.

"Have you seen Marco?" he asked.

She nodded slightly. "He seems to be doing well. He really likes his aunt, but I know he misses you."

Hector's mouth contorted, the edges pulling down hard. "I miss him, too."

"I'm so sorry, Hector," she told him, putting her hand atop his on the table.

"I know this," he said.

"Oh, there she is," Ynna heard from over her shoulder and turned to see two Carcer officers pointing in her direction.

Hector stood protectively as they strode over.

"Marina Hawkins?" one asked.

"Yes," she squeaked.

"Daddy paid your bounty, time to go," he said.

She looked at him with pure puzzlement. "I just got here."

"Well, you're getting out," he said impatiently. "Way of the world, Princess."

She turned to Hector, who wore a broad smile on his face. "I tell you."

"You did," she said in disbelief.

"Go find your purpose," he said and gave her a hug that she knew to be farewell.

"I'll get you out of here someday," she assured him, and for a reason she couldn't quite understand, she believed it.

Hector nodded. "I know you will."

She followed the guards back the way she had come and went through the whole process she had just been through in reverse. She was given back her clothes and ushered into another transport. A guard pointed to a screen at the rear of the vehicle, and she slid down the long seat to be close to it.

Her father's face appeared in a pre-recorded message. "Ynna, just when I think you can't sink any lower, you do this to me. The shame you have brought on your family can never be washed off. Don't think that by freeing you, I want anything to do with you. I simply couldn't have my daughter be known as a prisoner. Get your life together and try not to sully my reputation any further."

The screen went black. Ynna didn't care what he had to say, and the words didn't land. She only cared that she was free.

She checked her pockets to find that Carcer had confiscated all she had taken from the house.

Two more prisoners were loaded in, and a guard began to shut the door behind them.

"Excuse me," Ynna said.

The guard grunted and stuck his head back in the transport. "What?"

"Where is this going?" she asked.

"You three all have residences on file in Redwood Point, where do you think you're going?" He slid the door closed.

"Shit," Ynna muttered.

"You want more?" one of the five thugs asked her and laughed maniacally. "Killian was right about her."

It hadn't taken long after she got off the transport for the men to find her. At first, she had hoped it was random, but at the mention of Killian's name, she knew he must have found out that the bounty had been paid and sent teams out into the street to find her.

As she attempted to get up, one of the broad men smashed his foot on her already broken hand. She screamed as the pain shot through her, the sound of her voice mixing with that of the bones in her fingers cracking.

"Now, he told you not to come back here," the man said, looming over her. He pulled a crowbar out from under his denim jacket.

"Hey!" a voice shouted from across the street.

Most of the people in this neighborhood were happy to turn

a blind eye to violence, and Ynna was shocked to hear anyone was interceding.

The thugs turned. "You don't want any part of this, fancy boy."

Ynna looked up to see a delicate-looking man in a fine suit with a hatbox tucked under one arm walking toward them. He didn't look like a fighter, and she had no idea why he was getting involved.

One of the thugs walked toward him, chest puffed up in a show of intimidation.

The delicate man kept walking and whispered something in the brute's ear.

He turned and hustled over to the leader, clearly repeating whatever he had been told.

"We don't want any trouble, but we better not see her around here anymore," the thug said and turned to spit on Ynna. She tried to block her face with a limp hand.

The thugs disappeared up the street as the man approached. He extended a hand. "You seem to be in need of some assistance."

"Yeah, thank you for that," she said, looking at him with utter confusion.

"It was a great pleasure," he said and pointed to her hand. "We will need to do something about that. Would you like to come with me?"

Ynna snorted. "What are you? Some kind of serial killer?"

"Oh, my, no," he said, offended. "I'm a medical man. My name is Terrence, though my friends call me Grimy."

"Grimy, I get it," she said, looking him over. "Clever."

"Terribly," he said with a scoff.

"Where will we go?" she asked.

Though she was smart enough not to trust the situation, something about the man made her feel comfortable. Also, he had just saved her life, and she had nowhere else to go, so she was comfortable entertaining the idea.

"We have a safe house," he told her in a hushed tone. "I work with some people for the betterment of the world, and we are currently looking for new members. Something tells me you could use some new friends."

She thought about her life and what Hector had said to her.

"Yes," she agreed. "I could."

Grimy smiled at her.

IN THE MIDDLE OF DOWNTOWN, hidden behind a false wall in an apartment complex, Grimy was working on Ynna's wounds as an old man entered the room.

"New blood?" the man asked as he looked at her. He had an unkempt white beard and glass plate where one of his eyes should be.

"I'm Burn," the man said.

"Ynna," she said, extending her good hand. His natural eye appraised her.

"Looks like you got bucked from your old life," Burn said with a grin from beneath his beard. "But I think I have a new saddle that will suit you just right."

"Do we get to fuck with Carcer?" Ynna asked.

Burn lit a long, hand-rolled cigarette. "Oh, yes. But that's only part of it."

Ynna smiled.

NOTE TO THE READER

Thanks for reading Deadly in Pink: A Cyberpunk Novella. If you enjoyed the book, please leave a review, it is incredibly helpful to authors. Reviews are one of the ways in which people can discover new work and help me to create more of it. I read all the reviews and love to hear what people think of my work. Thanks again for reading.

For more information and bonus content, visit Thuto-World.com

AUTHOR BIO

Matthew A. Goodwin has been writing about spaceships, dragons, and adventures since he was twelve years old. His passion for fantasy began when he discovered a boxed set of the Hobbit radio drama on cassette tape in his school's library at the age of seven. He fell in love with fantasy worlds and soon discovered D&D and Warhammer miniatures.

Not wanting to be limited by worlds designed by others, he created Thutopia (now called the Thuton Empire), a fantasy world of his own that he still writes about to this day.

Like many kids with an affinity for fantasy, a love of science fiction soon followed. He loved sweeping space operas and gritty cyberpunk stories that asked questions about man's relationship to technology. That led him to write his first published work, Into Neon: A Cyberpunk Saga, which takes place in a larger science fiction universe.

He has a passion for travel and wildlife, and when he is not off trying to see the world, he lives in San Francisco with his wife and son.

Printed in Great Britain
by Amazon